The Elephant Whisperer's Daughter

Nadya Radonich

First published in Far North Queensland, 2025 by Bowerbird Publishing

ISBN 978 1 7642319 3 0 (print)
ISBN 978 1 7642319 4 7 (ebook)

The Elephant Whisperer's Daughter
By Nadya Radonich

Cover & Interior Design: Crystal Leonardi
Editing: Crystal Leonardi

Distributed by Bowerbird Publishing
Available in National Library of Australia

Bowerbird Publishing
Julatten, Queensland, Australia
www.crystalleonardi.com

Proudly 100% Australian owned, operated & produced.

To my Mum and Dad, who took me everywhere.
In loving memory of my Grandfather, who loved to read.

CONTENTS

Prelude

My name is Maggie. Margaret Dawn Jones, to nobody but my mother when she thought I was misbehaving.

I was born in an air raid shelter, just as the aeroplanes were creeping across the sky in the dark, during The Blitz, WWII. The air outside was hushed in anxious anticipation, the kind of silence that only wartime England knew.

My mother readied herself for bed - unaware she was also readying herself for me. She had been blessed with cascades of brown hair, which was just past her shoulders at the time. After she brushed her springy, ruddy waves, she twisted them into a perfect plait over her shoulder. I must have given her a firm indication that I was ready to join her as she rose from her dressing table clutching her round belly, quivering as a thousand feelings flooded her at once.

The air raid shelter was in our garden. My mother rushed into her slippers, pulled on her dressing gown and slunk across the wet lawn as the first siren blared. She found her way to the shelter by striking a match. Once inside, she found the only storm light in the shelter and quickly struck the wick with another match.

"Just a few more minutes, my love," she whispered to her

belly while the shelter rattled as another bomb was dropped in the distance. "Just a few more minutes and he'll be here."

I had always thought I was quite mad to choose to be born in the middle of an air raid; but my father always said that I would not be who I am today if I had picked any other time. My mother tells me the story of the day I was born on my birthday every year. She remembers it well, she says.

I opened my eyes to the sound of my own cry, ringing out and bouncing off the shelter's walls. My vision was blurred, as most newborns' eyes must be. I squinted as I searched my new surroundings. I heard my mother laughing and crying simultaneously as she wiped my cloudy eyes with the base of her thumb. Then a frantic knock at the shelter door announced the arrival of my father.

"Mary?" He said anxiously, "Mary, are you alright? Can I come in?"

"Come in!" My mother cried with exhausted joy.

The door burst open, and my new eyes searched for where the noise had come from. My father stood in the doorway, and he staggered forward, struck to the heart to see my mother and me there, all alone in the dark.

"Where's the doctor?" My father breathed, the smile in his voice betraying the baffled expression on his face.

"Didn't need him in the end." My mother said, her voice matching my father's as she returned her loving smile down to me, stroking my tiny hand. My milky eyes followed her gaze as she raked me from my little toes to the whisps of brown hair.

My father staggered still further toward us, and when he found his feet, he collapsed beside us. I heard the sound of kissing, and looked up to see him kissing my mother's temple; his hand trembled as it touched my tiny head. His hand was cold, but a surge of electricity, which must have been the instant connection between us, warmed us both.

"Oh, Mary…" My father sighed, "She's beautiful, my love."

"Hmm," My mother agreed lovingly, and turned to look down at me. "She is, isn't she?"

I squinted, and my tiny hand brushed my father's chin. His hand was so much bigger than my own, and his touch, still so new and strange to me, made me frown with deep curiosity. I must have looked a little funny, for I saw my parents' faces light up with silent laughter, full of love for me, as I must have been for them, even if I didn't know it yet.

"We'll call her Margaret." My father whispered in my mother's ear, resting his head on her shoulder as he gazed, besotted, at me. "After your mother."

"Margaret…" My mother whispered as she kissed my cheek. I screwed up my face and squirmed in protest at being held so close when all I wanted was to run; I think I must have wanted to run, my legs were kicking like fury from the moment I drew breath.

NADYA RADONICH

PART 1

TEN YEARS LATER, BURMA

NADYA RADONICH

CHAPTER 1

WWII had ended, and the promise of a new decade and a journey to a new country seemed to make all the terrible things the war had left in its wake disappear. The air outside our home was thick with London fog, the war still lingering in the cracks of our quiet, battered home. My father was excited. He had been born with a strong heart and spirit, and legs kicking, like me, ready for adventure.

We were bound for the wilds of Burma, my parents and I. My father felt it was time for a fresh start.

"It'll be a long journey." My father said to my mother one night, not long before we began that journey.

"One you've been aching for your whole life, I should think." My mother purred as a smile full of love spread across her face. "You've never liked staying in one place for very long."

"Well, it's high time we let Mags out to see the world," My father said, half to himself. "She's read too many books not to start itching. The itch starting at the feet, I shouldn't wonder."

My father bent to my mother, who was much shorter than he, and kissed her. My mother gave a soft chuckle of agreement. Then I saw her make a face, as one does when about to sneeze, and, plucking her handkerchief from her pocket, she swept into a violent attack. She always sounded a little like a fairy with a head cold when she sneezed.

"You alright?" Asked my father softly.

"Yes." My mother replied, interrupted by a further assault from her nose. "Ugh! The sooner we leave this wretched country and its weather, the better!"

I rolled my eyes and went to my father's study; I wanted to know more about the possibilities of animals and places we might see in Burma.

A long journey, one I had always wanted to take. My father was a writer and nature conservationist, known to his close friends as 'the elephant whisperer'. He kept journals, mostly. He was born in India to a British mother and father; his father, my grandfather, was a game hunter, and my father had been to almost every exotic country known to man.

There was a globe in my father's study. I thought about it as we ascended the gangplank. The last time I saw that globe, my father had it turned to Singapore. He obliged me by spinning it around, having caught me staring and hearing my question; *I wonder where Singapore is?*

He traced a line from England, down the bright blue

paint representing the vast ocean, to a little patch beside a larger patch, which bore the name 'Singapore'. It was quite an old globe; the paper on which all the seas and countries were painted was torn in places, the letters partly scratched away on Australia and China.

"Then from there, we'll go by boat again, to Burma." He pointed, whispering with excitement in his voice.

I felt my chest give an excited heave as I drew an excited breath. For some reason, still unclear to me today, the idea of going to a far-off place was the most exhilarating thing that could ever happen to me.

My father was a brave man and an adventurer, and it always surprised me that the war hadn't frightened or scarred him as it had so many others. He always said that he and I shared an adventurous spirit.

He had never been to Burma, but he could speak the language. He spoke a few languages apart from his own, which was one of the many things I admired about him.

The day arrived for us to leave our motherland, England. I remember standing at the London docks, the smell of salt air and steam from the steamboats remains in my memory to this day. The ferry's whistle blew, quieting all the thoughts and memories that seemed to flood my mind as I stepped aboard. When the ferry moved, my heart gave a lurch of childish excitement, making me feel even younger than my 10 years.

I ran onto the deck, bent over the starboard bow, and watched as the ship churned the white seafoam, my heart fluttering in time with the water. I saw a shadow in the watery foam, *a dolphin*, said the little voice inside me, as a gasp of unbridled joy caught in my throat.

It was supper time, on the first Sunday of our first week on board. Our hosts, the crew on board the ferry, all hailed from Singapore and spoke in a tongue that my father had mastered rather beautifully. I had no idea what they were saying.

Well, I thought, *at least they're happy*. And they were, not one of them didn't have a smile on their face. At least, not until they saw my face when they served us our entrée, which looked suspiciously like dehydrated or fried cricket.

My mother made a face, too. I always knew something wasn't right if my mother made a face. Especially if she grimaced at food. And then there was my dear old Dad, gratefully and graciously tucking into his fried cricket. He had learned to ignore my mother's various expressions of disapproval to avoid conflict.

I could smell something else cooking. This time, it was fish, or crab; a sea creature of some description, mingled with the scent of every exotic spice I could name, and possibly a few I couldn't.

A lady in a sarong came out of the galley kitchen, wearing a smile that would thaw the coldest of hearts. I couldn't see any goose pimples, but we were already getting considerably nearer to the equator.

As she set down our supper, whole fish garnished with chilli and something I had never seen or heard of before called *coriander*, she put her hands together as though to pray. My father explained that the gesture was to wish us a good meal. And a good meal it was. I went to my hammock feeling quite replete. My mother, on the other hand, did not; unused to exotic spices, she spent much of the night vomiting and racing to the bathroom, the description of which is hard to explain. I believe it was a little more than something resembling a bucket.

In the morning, I woke to the sound of low-flying seagulls and emerged from our cabin. We must have been close to land. My father followed, fighting the gentle breeze to light his cigarette. My eyes raked him slowly as I wondered where Mummy was and, hearing my unspoken question, he asked me, "Do you think you'll like living abroad, Mags?"

Mags was his pet name for me. I was christened Margaret after my grandmother.

"Yes," I timidly replied. "I think so."

"Ah, we're going to visit some beautiful places." He

said reminiscently. Then, with one of his lopsided smiles, he added, "You'll love it."

That night, my mother didn't join us for dinner. My father and I took our supper on deck, where I noticed his far-off look; as an adventurer at heart, he always looked distracted, but that night was different.

I asked him what the matter was. He looked sideways at me, and a corner of his mouth curved, which I found quite alarming. I could usually read my father so well.

"There's going to be a baby in the family very soon." He said, somewhat mysteriously.

My mother was having another baby. *Well, that explains a lot,* I thought.

The rest of our journey to Singapore passed quite uneventfully. My father spent his days working at his typewriter and journal in turns, and my mother spent hers reclining and reading, finding her sea legs, of which she was not in possession when we first left London.

I played chess a lot, sometimes with my father, sometimes on my own. When I played on my own, I would look to the other side of the board and wonder what age my new sibling should be when I started teaching them to play.

The air when we arrived in Singapore was heavy, like a

hammock filled with all the goose feathers from every pillow in the world. It felt like it could rain at any moment, but the sky was free of clouds, save the ones of smog and dust.

My father gripped my hand, and I looked up as he did so. He was smiling. His smile always enhanced his generous mouth.

"Well, then!" He enthused, "Let the adventure commence."

"Oh, thank goodness." My mother exhaled, obviously relieved to see a funny little tricycle attached to a carriage.

"Hello, Mr. Jones!" Said the transport driver, who was in charge of what I quickly learned was called a *rickshaw*. "I hope you had a good trip!"

The first thing I noticed about our driver was his beaming, friendly smile, which was rare in England. It was one of those smiles that you couldn't help but smile back at, no matter your mood at the time.

My father helped Mummy onto the rickshaw first, and I followed soon after. My father's hands grabbed me around the middle, and he lifted me up. I remember being raised in the air in that fleeting moment, seeing a vast rice farm in the distance; I recognised them from the illustrations in many of my father's books.

Can a person really see that far? I wondered, amazed at my eyesight. *Are we really this close to a rice field?*

Our friendly guide swung a leg over the seat of his tricycle, like a rider mounting a horse. I turned to look over my shoulder and watched as the Singapore docks stretched away into the distance.

I turned to my mother. She was smiling now, and put one arm around my shoulder and a hand on the crook of my arm, almost as if she was holding onto me for dear life. Still, at least she was smiling.

I had never ridden in anything other than a London cab. While the rickshaw wobbled slightly as it weaved its way through the traffic to which I was also unaccustomed, somehow tucked up in this funny little vehicle, I felt much safer than I perhaps might if I were riding a bicycle through the streets of Singapore.

As we rode along, I closed my eyes. We swerved, turned corners and dipped into the craters in the road. I had a strange, wonderful feeling as though I was flying through the air like one of the seagulls we had left behind at the London docks.

The sound of motorcycles and car horns filled the air around me. With my eyes still closed, I could imagine a smile on just about everyone's faces because even when they shouted at one another, they still sounded happy.

I heard the sound of a match striking, and smiled as the scent of my father's tobacco filled my nostrils. Then I heard our driver shouting happily in conversation with my father, above the traffic noise. He said something about the bungalow where we would stay for the night before going to Burma. He told my father it was small, but comfortable. "Very English!" He said.

I had never wanted to keep my eyes closed before, especially not whilst on a new and exciting adventure. But something about the smells and sounds made me wish I were blind. Needless to say, that made me open my eyes faster than I had closed them. I looked at my mother. She seemed to have settled considerably and was reading from Agatha Christie's Poirot.

When I finally opened my eyes, I observed a quaint fruit and vegetable stall on a corner. Bunches of bananas hung from a beam in the tin ceiling like Christmas bunting. There were green fruits laid out in a bowl made of walnut, which my father identified as custard apples, and, lined up to create a neat border around the bench where all the fruit was laid, were whole coconuts.

My father tapped our friendly guide on the shoulder. He stopped the cart, and we got out.

My father greeted the lady vendor in warm tones of the local dialect. She nodded and handed him a large bunch of yellow and green bananas, as well as a single custard apple, for which he paid her with the few coins he had in his trousers pocket.

He must have asked her for a small knife, as she handed him one. He sliced the custard apple in half so my mother and

I could share it.

"What do you think, Mags? Do you like it?" He asked.

I licked my lips. I could taste custard; *hence the name*, I supposed, and honey, and, despite its texture of wet cotton wool, it was one of the sweetest, most delicious fruits I had ever eaten.

My father kissed my mother on the lips. My mother, too, must have enjoyed the fresh cotton wool disguised as fruit, for she stole another kiss. I had never seen them so happy. From that moment, London, England, stopped being my home.

CHAPTER 2

Very English our bungalow was not; nor was it a bungalow. It was more like a two-story building with rooms above a butcher, a florist, or a café. It was a slender building with a tin shed on either side.

I could hear hens clucking. So, one of the sheds was a chicken coop. The other shed was filled with bamboo. I wondered why on earth anyone would need that much bamboo. Perhaps they made their furniture with it, or sold it at a market; I imagined I would find out soon enough.

My nose began to tingle again. This time, it was the smell of fresh spices and coconut-something cooking.

"My daughter, she make your lunch." Our driver explained.

Suddenly, "Papa! Papa!"

A girl around my age burst out of the house, angrily waving a wooden spoon. Frustrated Malay quickly followed her exclamations of 'Papa'. Our driver stealthily took the wooden spoon from the girl's grasp and spoke soothingly to her.

My parents gathered around me as we listened to what I assumed was our driver asking his daughter for an explanation as to why she was so upset. The girl whispered her answer. Our guide turned to us apologetically, "One moment, please, sorry."

"What on *earth* is happening?" My mother said, turning a baffled look to my father.

For a moment, my father didn't speak. Then, "I *think* a monkey might have stolen the remains of the last coconut."

"Oh!" Gasped my mother.

My father was right. No sooner had our driver entered the house with his daughter, than a monkey scurried out, climbed the plumbing and pitter-pattered across the roof, and leapt from roof to coconut palm, like a gymnastics expert.

My father snorted. It was always instantly infectious when he laughed, and everyone was soon bursting with laughter, even the driver's daughter.

After dinner, I snuck into the kitchen, where our driver's daughter was washing up. She was standing on a small wooden stool, and singing a cheerful Burmese tune, which, while I was curious to know the words, I was content to listen.

"Hello," I said, "What's your name?"

"My name Mae," Said the girl in broken English, "You?"

"I'm Maggie!" I said happily. "Our names are almost the

same… Well, they both start with the letter M, anyway."

Mae smiled shyly at me and giggled. I answered her with a similarly shy giggle as I glanced around the room in search of a tea towel.

"You dry?" She asked, nodding at the plate in her hand.

I saw the growing pile of dishes to my right, and nodded keenly. Suddenly, Mae started telling me her life story. She didn't have very good English, but her tone was enthusiastic.

She had lost her mother when she was very young, but said she quite liked taking charge of things like her Mama used to. She went to work with Papa sometimes at the rice fields further out of the city.

I smiled, and could suddenly sense my father watching us. I could even tell he was smiling his lopsided smile, the one he reserved for listening to a story that made his own pale in comparison.

After everyone had gone to bed, I lay awake; the excitement of our almost month-long journey and our arrival, meeting Mae and the adventures of the monkey thief were more exciting than any of the stories in any of the books I had read.

Now my mind was racing in time with the t*ap, tap, tap* of my father's fingers on his typewriter. I closed my eyes, and the full picture of my father working at his desk appeared. He typed quite quickly and usually worked best with the body of a ballpoint pen between his teeth. At home, his desk was piled with notebooks, notepads and paper; I wondered if it was now, and I smiled. It probably was.

The clicking of the typewriter's keys and the warm, heavy air I was unaccustomed to, sent me into a dreamlike state. As my eyes began to close, I took an unconscious note of the walls made of roughly applied cement and the windows with sweet bamboo shutters painted white.

CHAPTER 3

In the morning, the house was already a hive of activity. I was woken by the strange aroma of buffalo dung and fried eggs with chilli and oyster sauce. I could hear our driver, whose name, I learned later, was Pang, and Mae chatting frantically in the kitchen.

Then came two voices whose accent and conversation I recognised. My father and mother were talking, seemingly quite cheerfully, to another man. He was English, but as far as I knew, I hadn't met him before. I figured he was a photographer when my mother said, "Go on, then. Let's see the new camera!"

I felt as keen to see his new camera as my mother so I hurried downstairs. I judged my parent's friend as a good-natured man from the brightness of his eyes and the kindness of his smile. He must have heard me coming, as he turned before I had left the stairwell.

"Ah!" he said happily, "You must be the famous Mags. If I can call you that?"

I nodded.

"Don't be shy, Mags." Said my mother reassuringly. "This is George. He's coming to Burma with us."

I turned to George. "It's very nice to meet you, Mr....?" I said, shyly.

"Oh," replied George, "Just call me George. Everyone does."

I made up my mind then to like George. We would be safe on our adventure with him. He had a kind, unusual face, a little like an otter, with light brown tight curls on his head and a thin moustache that disappeared into his friendly smile.

George's camera looked quite expensive. It was small and square, like a pair of binoculars with a beak. I thought he must have acquired it recently, or was just so proud of it that he polished it each time he used it, for it sparkled as though it had its own Hollywood smile.

"Have you ever seen a tiger, Maggie?" He asked me, as if seeing a tiger was the only thing I should ever want to do in my entire life.

"No." I replied excitedly.

"Just you wait!" He said, nodding at me. "If you've ever heard them called the king of the jungle… I tell you… it's not true until you see them with your own eyes."

Suddenly, I remembered the tiger's head in my grandfather's sitting room. It was mounted proudly above the fireplace, its green eyes made of glass blazing like wildfire, its mouth open as if it would swallow you up if you dared enter.

I was looking forward to seeing tigers that were alive. I was sure they didn't look as dangerous in their natural environment, admired from afar, not being hunted by people like my grandfather.

Pang led us out to where his tuk-tuk was parked, and there, beside it, towering over it like a headmaster might tower over a young student, was an enormous Range Rover.

"Isn't she a beauty!" George exclaimed, marching over to the vehicle and patting it as if greeting a close chum, "You'll never guess. She came all the way from England with me!"

"Well," said my father ruefully, "If ever anyone needed proof you were crackers…"

George chuckled. "Come on, then!" He said, and marched over to me, lifting me as if I were as light as a feather and carried me to the back of the Range Rover. "Wilds of Burma, here comes Princess Mags and her friend, Princess Mae!"

I looked over my shoulder. My father was helping my mother into the seat behind me. They sat together, and Mae and I were side-by-side. We smiled at each other. Suddenly, Mae seemed to become a child again; she had looked so grown up when I first saw her that I thought she was much older than I was, even though I knew we were the same age.

We grabbed each other's hands and looked at one

another with terrified excitement. I wondered if we were thinking the same thing, hoping the tigers wouldn't get close enough to see us as food.

CHAPTER 4

My mother had been quiet for most of the journey thus far. I wondered if she was ill, or if perhaps she didn't want another baby. I could see no reason that either thing should be the case; she didn't look sick, and she and my father seemed happy at the beginning of the journey. She was usually quiet anyway, I reasoned, but it was troubling that she and my father had spoken so little.

They smiled at each other briefly, and my father kissed my mother's hand as if to reassure her; then he struck a match and lit a cigarette.

I don't remember a great deal about our journey through Singapore. I must have fallen asleep; the motion of slow-travelling cars always seemed to relax me, but I do remember being stuck in traffic as we entered the city centre. It was a market day, and the motor cars, bicycles, and tuk-tuk's had all slowed almost to a complete halt. People blew their horns and shouted, and that, along with the chatter of the thousands of people at the market, must have been the lullaby that did it for me.

I woke to find that we were making a slow ascent up a winding road. The hushed tones of the adults in conversation pulled me slowly out of the land of dreams, and I looked around to find that Mae and my mother were still fast asleep.

"It's a marvelous place," George said. "Pang here, and I, have been a few times. They do so much conservation work…" Then, a little louder, he turned to me and said, "How would you like to see elephants, Lady Mags?"

"Are we going to see elephants?" I exclaimed.

"Yes, we are, my love." Said my father. "And elephants have a very good memory. Once they meet you, they will never forget you."

I was so excited by this that I could feel a lump in my throat, and tears in my eyes. Then I heard my mother's kind, soft laughter, "Oh, Mags, don't be silly." Sympathetically, she took her handkerchief from her breast pocket and dabbed my eyes, adding, "Don't *cry*."

"Here," said Pang, passing something over his shoulder, "Barley sweet. It make you feel better, Mags."

"Where in the name of God did you come by that, Pang?" Asked George in surprised amusement.

"I took many barley sugars from British soldiers when war was on. Had to keep something from Japanese bastards!" Pang replied.

My mother gasped sharply and covered Mae's and my

ears quickly. My father, George, and Pang all laughed.

From the corner of my eye, I caught a glimpse of the flicking tail of a cow. She had her back to us and was hidden by tall grass and the young bamboo trees that lined the dusty trail.

"Oh, Mags, look!" gasped my mother, excitedly. She pointed skyward, gathering me up with one arm.

I obliged. A family of macaques gathered in the higher branches of a coconut palm; the two youngsters were swinging, one by a leg, the other by his tail from the branch. Their parents took turns grooming each other. George whisked out his camera and snapped the scene, and my father stood up with his binoculars at the ready, always eager to get a closer look. "Ah, to be *this* close!" he breathed.

"Remarkable, isn't it?" said George.

I caught sight of Mae. She had picked up the cigarette that had surreptitiously fallen from my father's hand when he excitedly rose to his feet. She put it to her lips and was about to inhale. "Mae!" Shouted Pang, followed by a cacophony of stern-sounding Malay.

Mae put her finger to her lips to make sure I was quiet. I smiled at her. I admired her spirit, but at the same time, the idea of a child my age puffing on a cigarette, which I assumed only adults did, shocked me.

Mr. Pang's angry tones must have frightened our monkey

friends away, for my father had resumed his seat behind me, and when I looked up, the monkeys had vanished. We could still hear them chattering however, their voices echoing through the jungle.

"Ah, well," said Pang reflectively. "At least they didn't take your cigarette, Mr. Jones."

Everyone laughed, and we continued up the hill in a plume of engine smoke.

It was dark when we arrived in the Burmese countryside, and even in the dark, I could see that my mother was a funny shade of greyish-green; nauseated by travel, tiredness, pollution and pregnancy, my father had to lift her from the Range Rover. She bent over the other side of the car and exploded with violent illness. My father stood by, holding my mother upright, reassuring her. I stood frozen to the spot; I had never seen a person being sick, and it was pretty awful.

We were staying at a small campsite, and our home for the duration of our stay was three large tents; one for my parents and me, one for Mae and Pang, and the other for George.

"I-I'm sorry," my mother said, yawning, "I think I'll have to hit the hay soon."

"Of course," said George, kindly, "We understand, of course."

My father ushered my mother to a tent conveniently sheltered by bamboo and coconut palms.

Later, I lay awake, listening to my father's fingers working quickly at his typewriter. He was close enough that I could hear each time he took a long drag on his cigarette, coughing at almost every second exhalation. *Tap, tap, tap,* hacking, painful cough. I huffed and tossed off the thin coverlet. Swinging my legs over my hammock, I stood up, hoping neither of my parents would hear me tiptoeing across the rug of woven coconut fibre.

I opened the tent, and for a moment I felt as if I was at home in England, opening the curtains in my bedroom. But the clear, star-scattered night sky and lovely, clear, warm air, greeted me like someone giving me a lingering hug. I closed my eyes and inhaled deeply. Then I heard the sound of shuffling footsteps behind me. Then *snap,* the owner of the footsteps must have stepped on a twig, and I cracked my eyes open and turned sharply.

"Oh!" I gasped, shocked.

Mae was standing there, her arms crossed to cover her bare nipples. My eyes grew wide with shock. Then they travelled swiftly downward. She quickly cupped her nether regions to hide them from me.

"What are you *doing?!*" I hissed, unable to hide my comprehension of modesty, which Mae clearly didn't share, or care, it seemed.

"You swim?" She asked innocently.

"No!" I exclaimed, then more calmly I said, "Well, not naked anyway!"

Mae shrugged. "It's okay," she said, "Just keep shirt on."

I looked down at my shirt. It was a pristine, white linen, embroidered with little blue and yellow violets. I didn't think my mother would thank me for diving into what could be filthy water to swim in.

The bubbles tickled my face as I dived in; the water was warm, but cold enough to cool our hot, sticky skin. A decent wave splashed me in the face when I came up for air. Mae giggled; she pushed more water toward me, and I squealed. I splashed her back and we both burst into shrieking laughter. The monkeys we had seen earlier that day must have heard us, because they called out as if they were squealing with delight along with us. I don't know how long we played in the water, but I knew I never wanted to stop.

CHAPTER 5

"Margaret?"

My mother's horrified exclamation echoed down the hill as I imagined her voice rippling in the water like an angered god; "What on *earth* do you think you're doing? Get out and come here at once!"

Mae and I stood, wrapped in sarongs, facing four adult faces towering over us. With his hands clenched behind his back, Pang stalked up to Mae. Not quite shouting, he said something to her in their language.

"I'm sorry, Papa," Mae replied in English. She was quite upset.

Mr. Pang barked at her again, and I was sure he said, "No, you're not!"

"Stealing Mr. Jones's cigarettes! Swimming naked with Mr. Jones's daughter! What's gotten into you?"

Mae buried her head in her hands and began to sob. Mr. Pang made a sound of disapproval and snatched Mae's hands away from her; he gripped them so tightly that they blushed beneath his.

"Never do this again!" he growled, "You understand? Never!"

I turned to my parents. My mother looked kindly at Mae, as if she would happily adopt her and take her back to England with us.

Mae bowed her head.

I had expected something like stubbornness or defiance from her, but when she looked up, I saw only obedience and respect for her father in her expression. I wondered if the apparent seriousness of what Mae had done would be enough to cause Mr. Pang to stop Mae and me from being friends, but then Mae glanced sideways at me, and the stubborn defiance I had been looking for, twinkled in her eyes.

"Right," my father sighed, calm enough to take charge of the situation, and all too aware that Mr. Pang was anything but calm. "I think we should all be in bed. You two young ladies, go change into your night dresses, and straight to bed."

So, straight to bed we went. But not for long. I couldn't sleep. I didn't like the thought of Mae being punished for something that was innocent, even by British standards; so, at my own risk, and likely Mae's, too, I crept from my camp bed and tiptoed barefoot toward Mae and Mr. Pang's tent.

This time, I could hear the call of monkeys and the hoot of a lonely owl. Close to the camp, a man was asleep, sitting up, with his hands resting on a large machete. Beside him, there was a rifle similar to one I had seen mounted on the wall of my grandfather's sitting room. I supposed he was there to guard us from predatory animals or other men with machetes.

As peculiarly as I had found Mae standing naked behind me, I saw her now lying in the dirt with her arms at full wingspan, staring up at the stars and humming something in Malay.

"What are you doing?" I whispered.

"Singing," Mae replied, mockingly.

"What song is it?"

She frowned as if surprised that I didn't know. She started her song again, more slowly, and then I realised it was 'Twinkle, Twinkle, Little Star.'

"Where did you learn that song?"

"Mr. George teach me," she added cheerfully, "I translate you."

"Come." she said, patting the ground beside her, "I teach you."

I lay beside her as she continued singing, encouraging me to pick up the language by copying her. This I achieved, and we sang together in a tuneful whisper so that the adults wouldn't hear us.

"I'm sorry I got you into trouble," I said a moment later, but part of me wondered if it should be Mae apologising, and not me.

Mae shrugged and gave me a kind smile. "It's okay," she said, "not your fault."

We must have fallen asleep then, because whether or not we spoke anymore after our apologies, I can't recall. I woke at early dawn to the collective shouts of my parents and Mr. Pang. With leaves in my hair, I sat up, stretched and yawned. Blinking sleepily in the dusky pink haze of the sunrise, I saw the tall silhouette of my father marching toward me.

"There you are," he sighed with both exasperation and relief.

Mae roused from her deep sleep, and my father brushed us both down, fussily picking at the bits of earth and flora on our clothes and hair.

"Come on," he said, "Time for breakfast."

Our breakfast that morning was not exotic. Porridge was porridge; and even if it was traditional in Scotland, it was nothing to get excited about.

I observed George with a sideways stare as he examined his camera. He was squinting, one eye shut more tightly than the other, lips pouting at an odd angle, making sure that his photographic machine was in perfect focus to capture the right animal at just the right moment.

"It's mating season, Lady Mags," said George, knowing by now that I quite liked being called 'Lady'. "Do you know what that means?"

"For goodness' sake, George!" my mother shrieked playfully, "Maggie is ten years old, of course she doesn't..."

"It means the elephants are making babies!" Mae added mischievously.

She giggled into her hands, which made me laugh, then ducked and slunk away, covering her head to avoid her father's hand, which was raised and swinging for her, more in play than in discipline.

My father carried me on his back to the Land Rover, making a clopping sound with his tongue in his cheek, my valiant chestnut Charger.

We drove deeper into the Burmese jungle with a newly familiar chorus of birds and monkeys calling to each other. When I suddenly heard the trumpeting of a small herd of elephants, I knew we were close. As we slowed as to not disturb the magnificent sight, some of the herd played in the water, making short puffing sounds with their trunks, followed by water spurts.

We left 'The Rover', as George called it, at the top of a hill so we could observe the waterhole from above. True to his nature, my father rose eagerly to his feet, armed with binoculars to observe the large creatures at play. George, ready with his camera, began taking pictures enthusiastically. Mr. Pang instructed us to wait while he informed his relative, who managed the reserve, of our arrival.

We had brought with us an infestation of unwanted passengers in the shape of large mosquitoes; my mother was swatting them away madly while I noticed that my father bore a few angry red blotchy bite marks on the back of his neck. I knew enough about mosquitoes to know they carried diseases, but by the time I thought I should be concerned, Mr. Pang returned with his relative.

Introducing us, he said, "This my cousin. 'To'."

"*To?*" said George, seeming slightly confused, "What sort of a name is To? I thought you said you only had the one."

"George," my father hissed scoldingly, "Don't be so damned *ignorant*. To is the man's name, it doesn't mean he's also his cousin."

"Ah," said George, realising his foolishness, "Right you are, then. Sorry old chap."

Mr. To smiled and waved George's mistake away kindly. He beckoned to us, whispering something excitedly that we assumed to be, "Come, come!"

Mae and Mr. Pang disembarked, and gestured to the rest of us to follow.

"Come on then, Mags," said my mother cheerfully, "This is what we came here for!"

The path to the elephants was a steep descent, and it

wound like a spiral staircase paved with rocks and thickets of lush, green grass.

The trumpeting of elephants grew louder the closer we got, and when they came into sight, Mr. To motioned to us all to crouch down in the long grass.

"I go first," he whispered, "they know me. I calm them, then you come. Okay?"

With a collective nod from my father, George and Mr. Pang, Mr. To left us to inform the elephants of our arrival. He waved us down with a gap-toothed grin, giving one of the enormous animals a clap on the trunk.

"I say, To," said George, looking a little nervous as he approached the water's edge, "Isn't it mating season? Won't the ladies get a little…?" He made a honking sound, and Mae and I burst into a fit of childish laughter.

"No," snapped Mr. To with a little laughter lacing his voice. "Stupid man. Not mating season. Mating season finished already."

A young elephant approached and explored me with deep curiosity. The little stubbly hairs on his trunk tickled my nose and cheeks as he flicked it lazily over my whole face. I looked at my mother, who was making friends with the young mother of the herd; she was bathing her, smiling broadly as she spoke softly to the magnificent animal.

I heard the others talking to their new elephant friends.

My father was an animal lover, and I could have sworn I saw his eyes misting as he washed an elephant and fed it some of the whole cabbages and limbs of bamboo we had brought with us.

Mae and I squealed with joy as the elephants showered us with water from their trunks. Their trumpeting signaled their happiness at our being there to feed, wash, and bond with them.

My parents danced under a fountain tinted with hundreds of tiny rainbows that the matriarch elephant made for them; she held her trunk high in the air and seemed to strike a pose, with one front foot held up daintily. This moment reminded me of the time I watched my parents dance in the streets of London when the war ended, along with many other happy couples. They didn't look half as happy, even then, as they did now, dancing under their rainbow elephant fountain.

CHAPTER 6

In the days after our first meeting with the elephants, my bond with Mae deepened. We spent most of our time swimming in the elephant's waterhole; sometimes with the elephants, sometimes without them.

To distract my rebellious new friend from stealing any more of the grown-ups' cigarettes, I taught her Hide and Seek. She grasped the concept of the game quickly; it was the game's name in English that she initially didn't seem to understand.

My father and his colleagues continued what, at first, I thought was more of a hobby than serious work, but joining forces with Mr. To meant that they were undertaking serious conservation work.

My father was in his element. This, compared to fighting the enemies of Britain in the Second World War, was peaceful and healing to him as he had always been a placid man. My mother, on the other hand, while also enjoying the tranquility of this Buddhist country that was new to her, seemed to be growing rather bored. My father insisted that my mother, in her delicate condition, take complete rest. He said he had already made the mistake of forcing her to travel; the less activity she engaged in, the better.

The nights passed slowly. I drifted in and out of sleep, each time waking to a silence that felt too heavy, too still. Even the jungle seemed to hush its usual rustling.

When the sky finally began to brighten with the first morning light, the world outside the tent stirred again, and that was when I heard the panicked, whispering voices that belonged to my father, George and Mr. Pang. My father was in distress, but I could hear in his voice that he was trying to remain calm. They were gathered outside our tent, and I turned over in my camp bed to find that my mother was absent from her own. I tiptoed to a tent wall and pressed my ear to it to try to hear the whispering. There was talk of doctors, and something about the distance from here to the nearest hospital. I drew open the tent doors and peeped through. My father's hands were red with blood, which, from the conversation, I assumed belonged to my mother.

She had lost the baby, the little brother or sister that I had been told to expect. I could see that my father had been crying, something I had never seen before, and I knew he would hate to think I could see it now. I pulled the tent doors shut, closed my eyes, and tried to recall the Malay translation of 'Twinkle, Twinkle, Little Star'.

That night, I kept waking, expecting to hear my mother's voice or my father's cough from the tent. But all was quiet.

When morning came, George and Mr. Pang did their best to keep things normal for me. They made breakfast, told stories, and even let Mae and me help collect water from the river. And slowly, as mid-morning approached, a man arrived at the campsite.

He must have been a doctor, judging from the large black bag he took from his car; the car was smaller than our Range Rover, but large enough to brave the rough terrain of the nature reserve.

He was an Englishman. Not very tall, he was slightly round in the face and middle, with a balding head of grey hair. Round spectacles rested on the bridge of his nose.

I waited outside our tent as the doctor asked my father what had happened in the moments before my mother had lost the baby.

"Well…", I heard my father say, "my wife has always had a delicate constitution. I think the journey here might have had something to do with it…"

"Not so, Mr. Jones," said the doctor kindly, "If that were so, your wife would have miscarried days before now. Has she been unwell recently?"

There was a long silence before my father said, "Well… she's been a little tired, but once again, I just assumed it was from the journey here."

"May I see her?" asked the doctor.

My father's lips must have barely moved as he said, "Of course," for I only just understood.

I crept closer to the tent and looked inside. It was a large tent with two separate rooms, and I caught a glimpse of the two men as they moved from one part to the other; then I heard whispers, the voices belonging to my mother, father, and the doctor.

When my father spotted me from the corner of his eye, he came over and crouched down in front of me, holding me at arm's length. He explained as gently as he was able that I wasn't allowed to visit my mother just yet; she was very poorly, and I wouldn't want to see her in the state she was in. But, he explained, in no uncertain terms, she would get better; it would just take time.

The doctor, whose name was 'Banks', ordered that my mother be taken to the nearest hospital, to ensure the healthy completion of the miscarriage. I was to stay with George and Mr. Pang, my father said. He would be back in a day or so.

I felt tears welling in my eyes and at the back of my throat. I was sad for my parents' loss, and disappointed that I would not have a new sibling. My father dried my eyes, and reassured me that he knew how brave I was. He said, "You must remind yourself of just how brave you can be now."

Selfishly, I also felt relieved that our adventure hadn't come to a complete standstill. I didn't say this out loud; any ten-year-old should know what might, or might not be, a hurtful thing to say. I watched as Mr. Pang and my father helped my mother into the Range Rover; before he climbed in, my father took my head with both hands and kissed me. Never one for goodbyes, he didn't say a word; he knew the kiss, a parting gesture, would say all he needed to.

CHAPTER 7

In the days that followed, Mae and I played Hide and Seek and swam with the elephants. I found solace in the company of the gentle, loving animals, and my friendship with Mae was becoming more valuable to me than I had ever expected; I think Mae also found my presence comforting. She, like me, was an only child, and having grown up in a small village, had found it hard to make friends.

My parents were gone for longer than anyone had expected, and when they returned, while my mother appeared to have recovered relatively well, there was an odd silence between them. They were happy to see me, nonetheless, and greeted me as if I were unaware of what was happening between them.

My father worked like fury at his typewriter on the evening of my parents' return. He and my mother weren't talking much, which was odd because, they were happy as far as I could tell, but the strange tension between them could not be denied or ignored.

As I listened to my father's fingers tickling his typewriter keys, I observed with surprised concern that his usual cough, which I had heard the grown-ups call a 'smoker's cough' had changed - for the worse, it seemed.

When I woke the next morning, I heard the general sounds of preparation for the day ahead, and everyone sounded in high spirits. Today, we were going in search for tigers and, by the sound of it, we were heading deeper into the Burmese jungle.

We drove into a rainforest-like clearing; its ethereal beauty made it seem like a fairy's grotto, the emerald green leaves of the trees and long shoots of bamboo glistened in the rain. The air was alive with the sound of all walks of jungle life.

Mr. To informed us that the tigers were further inland, and so elusive that we mightn't even see any at all.

My mother, Mae, and I stayed safely behind my father and colleagues.

George locked and loaded his rifle. Should the unlikely need to use one arise, each of the men were armed. Our mission was to search for evidence of poachers in the area, and, should we find any such traps or baits, we were to dispose of them and report them to the appropriate authorities, whoever they were.

My mother initially objected to Mae and me accompanying them on such an expedition. Still, we insisted and besides, my father and Mr. Pang encouraged that women could be nature conservationists, too.

Mr. To knew a place where poachers set their traps. It was a short walk from where we were, through a small plantation of bamboo and then down into a little gully, but he warned us that we should be vigilant; the tigers were wild, and so, wildly unpredictable.

"Well!" said George, guns blazing, "unpredictable, they may be, but did they know I was going to do this?"

He began unbuttoning his trousers. My mother clapped a hand over my eyes; she must have covered Mae's eyes too because I heard a protestation of "Hey!" in English, followed by a few words of frustrated Malay.

Then, we heard a splashing sound, and childish laughter from Mr. Pang, George and my father. George and Mr. Pang had entered a small stream of fresh flowing water, to cool off.

Mummy tutted; "Really!" she huffed wryly.

My father coughed, then subsided; then again, more painfully. My mother gave him a look of concern, but I could tell she already knew what the matter was. Then they looked at each other, and the look seemed to say, This is just between us for now.

We set off on foot, in single file. Mr. Pang and Mr. To led

the way; my mother held Mae's and my hand, with my father in front of us and George behind us, each with rifles aiming in readiness to protect us.

I could hear my father's breathing. It was laboured as though he had just sprinted from here to wherever the next village was, and even I knew that was miles away.

There was a sudden rustling in the surrounding tall grass, and the men all aimed their rifles in different directions. We froze as we heard a gathering of voices in the distance. "Who's there?" my father shouted in Malay.

"What did he say?" I whispered to Mae.

The reply was a gunshot. Mr. To collapsed suddenly to the ground, and a wound spread quickly on his chest. He had been shot. Too much in agony to scream, he lay groaning in short bursts through gritted teeth.

Then, presumably the gunman, an armed national came charging through the jungle. Mae said he was a landowner, and we were trespassing. He demanded to know what we were doing there.

"We're not poachers!" said Mr. Pang in reassuring tones of their common language, "*Not poachers!*"

The man spoke threateningly, his narrowed eyes matching the tone of his voice.

"Prove it," Mae translated.

George took something carefully from his breast pocket:

a leather wallet that held his conservationist's license inside.

The man glanced at it, clearly realising he had made a terrible error.

"We're on your side," George said calmly, "Now, let us help our friend so we can leave you in peace."

"Okay," said our captor, raking us suspiciously, "You go quickly."

The man lowered his weapon, and with his eyes still resting suspiciously upon us, he disappeared. A moment later, he returned, carrying with what looked like a first-aid kit.

Mr. Pang and George were on their knees at Mr. To's side. Mr. Pang was cradling his cousin's head. Mr. To was in distress by now, and Mr. Pang spoke softly to him in their language, trying to calm him.

My father, with instruction from the landowner, tore open Mr. To's shirt, and the full extent of his injury became clear to us. All I can remember is the blood; a healthy red colour, spilling in waves from the bullet hole in Mr. To's chest. Then my mother omitted a short gasp, and the world obscured under the protective darkness of her hands once again over our eyes.

"Right," said George, like a soldier in full command of his troops, "Get him to the Rover. Quickly."

The Range Rover tossed and jolted us as George drove

at almost breakneck speed. Mr. To's beautiful skin, the colour of pale earth, had turned a funny greyish green by the strain and shock of his ordeal. Too weak to cry out now in pain, at least he seemed peaceful.

George had some experience with first aid; it was easy enough to staunch the bleeding, clean the wound, stitch and dress it, but they would need to work quickly.

"Evelyn?" said George, but my father was too dazed to respond immediately, "Evelyn! The exit wound. Can you see it?"

"Yes," my father replied, his voice shaking slightly, "Yes, but I-I don't know if it's near anything."

George stayed calm and checked where my father had both his hands stemming the blood flow, "It's alright," he said, wiping the anxious sweat from his top lip, "It's not near any vital organs. There's still time."

As we pulled up to camp, my father ordered my mother to, "Take the girls away, *now*." And my mother hurried us away to the safety of our tent.

We spent the next hours listening as my mother read to us; we had been reading Peter Pan, a story she had read to me many times, whose magic never failed to frighten away unpleasant images that bad dreams were made of.

It was ages before my father returned to us, his once-familiar smoker's cough now a harsh, unwelcome stranger, its sound unfamiliar and painful.

"Evelyn?" my mother quickly responded, "What happened? Is Mr. To alright?"

My father looked exhausted. Dark circles under his eyes, beads of sweat covered his face, and he had gone quite pale; he took his handkerchief from his breast pocket, mopped the sweat from his brow; "He'll survive", he said finally.

Later that night, I woke to find my mother shrugging into her dressing gown. It was made of crisp, white satin, embroidered with intricate purple violets and orange butterflies; my father was in his study in another part of the tent.

As usual, he was busy typing, but stopped abruptly upon my mother's arrival. She murmured kindly, "You can't go on keeping this from Mags forever. It's not fair to keep it secret. Especially if you get worse."

"That's not going to happen," he said, not unkindly; he had his cigarette between his teeth as he spoke, and I heard the jaunty ping of the typewriter carriage return as he moved it, "New treatments are being developed all the time. You've nothing to worry about, you or Mags."

Treatments for what? I wondered. I tried to think of all the ailments I knew that needed treatment. Needless to say, I couldn't think of any that didn't. It's curious; the less you know about something bad, the more anxious it makes you, but I knew my father's strength. He was an adventurer, a warrior. Whatever he needed to fight, he would do so bravely.

In the morning, things seemed rosier. Something about the promise of a new day made whatever had passed the day before evaporate in the sun rays of dawn.

I had woken, as usual, with the sparrows. Mae was already up and waiting for me. I could tell because I heard her singing, "Twinkle, Twinkle, Little Star," in soft tones of her native tongue.

"Hello, Maggies!" Mae chimed happily, clearly confusing my full name with my pet-name in her innocent, slight misunderstanding of English, "You come see!"

She took my hand and dragged me through the campground to her and Mr. Pang's tent, where Mr. To convalesced. When we got close, I could smell stale sweat and the body odour accompanying it.

Mae drew back the tent's curtains, and to my surprise, Mr. To was sitting upright in bed, listening to a little wireless radio, to what sounded like an important announcement.

When he saw Mae and me, he addressed Mae a little sternly, and I learned that her name was Mae Wen, for that is what he shouted before waving at the radio and barking an order at her.

She hurried over to the radio and turned up the volume, "This is our King, Maggie Jones," he said, rather proudly.

Mae spoke excitedly to him then, and at first Mr. To seemed to protest, but Mae applied pressure by way of begging, her hands clasped together like a deprived soul. Mr. To sighed, "Okay," he said in defeated English, "You ask for it," he warned.

He lifted his shirt. He was bandaged from the middle to the shoulder, which made him look a bit like an Egyptian mummy, but a friendlier one, surely there never was.

"Does it hurt?" I asked.

"No, Maggie Jones," he said, seeming touched. "I alive. That all that matter."

CHAPTER 8

Our mission the following day was to check the well-being of an orangutan family who, we had been told had a nest in the deepest part of the jungle's rainforest. Some of the females were expectant mothers. The mission would take us high into the Burmese mountains.

Rather like at home in England, the weather couldn't make up its mind to be clement. There was a drizzle at breakfast, then the sun appeared, and when we began the mountain climb in the Range Rover, it bucketed down. This, of course, didn't stop my father, Mr. Pang or George's enthusiasm of the expedition ahead. They all rode standing up as the rain pelted and soaked them through. My mother, Mae and I were sheltered by the tarpaulin hood of the vehicle. Mae and I were a little disheartened that our view from the mountain was obstructed in favour of remaining dry.

At last, we arrived near the top of the hill, and while it wasn't yet the tip of the mountain, we were nearer to the clouds than I had ever been before.

If the orangutans were nearby, they certainly knew how

to make themselves scarce. There was barely a sound, other than the usual twittering of birds, the call of a few monkey species, or the distant roar of tigers.

As I looked around in wonder, something caught my eye. A Burmese python was swinging from the vines of a tree; its body dipped in the middle, and its head raised, waiting, it looked like, at a bird's nest, for the right time to strike and sample the bird's offspring.

"Oh, Mags, look!" my father whispered excitedly.

He bent down and rested his hands, which were cold and soaked by the rain, on my shoulders. He pointed skywards. I looked up and there, nestled high in a tree, was a family of orangutans. The baby swung by one arm and one leg from a branch of the tree they were perched on; occasionally poking out his tongue, either to give his parents' cheek or testing the cool, sweet rain water.

"Isn't that *wonderful*, my darling?" my father whispered.

I looked up at him. My father wore a marvellous smile.

Mr. Pang was busy jotting down observations in his notepad; George took pictures, and my father started to clear the overgrowth of weeds and a few fallen branches to protect the orangutan's nesting area.

I noticed my mother watching my father with loving admiration. There was a longing sadness in her eyes. But, I wondered, why would she need to pine for him when he was right there in front of her?

Then, something magic happened. The baby orangutan climbed down from the tree and approached my father. It reached up like a small child who wanted to be held and made a grunting sound, the kind of sound a child makes when they don't immediately get what they want.

"Come on, then," my father insisted, opening his arms. The tiny orangutan jumped into my father's arms. We all gasped, unable to hide our amazement at what was unfolding.

Then, as suddenly as it had begun, the moment was over. The little primate gestured to get down so my father knelt and released the little creature from his clutches, and it scampered back up the tree to its family. Smiling, my mother's eyes were full of tears. My father smiled back at her, his own eyes twinkling with emotion. With hands on hips, he cocked his head and smiled up at the tree and watched the family of orangutans go about their day.

"Right," said George, upbeat, "That's that lot safe and sound. Nice to feel appreciated, isn't it?"

We all laughed and the whole forest seemed to join in the laughter, our symphony ringing out above the sound of drizzling rain.

We continued up the mountain on foot. The rain had eased to a trickle from the leaves on the trees to the forest floor, the humidity had risen, and the clouds, while still slightly weighted with precipitation, moved across the sky, now whiter in colour.

We worked together, clearing the forest of what few traps and other obstructions to the orangutan's habitat we could find; all of us now familiar enough with one another to work in companionable silence.

I remember feeling the temperature drop ever so slightly, the chill biting my skin, and my clothes clinging to me with the unpleasant warmth of sweat.

By the time we got back to camp at dusk, dark had almost set in. We set about lighting a fire and the lanterns that hung outside each of our tents. My mother boiled water so we could all have something hot to drink.

I watched my father peel the soaking wet shirt from his back. He bent over the fire and rubbed his hands together furiously to get warm.

When we were all comfortable and dry, my father and I sat side-by-side on a stump by the fire, sipping cocoa from ceramic camp mugs.

"We had these in our dugouts when the war was on, Mags." My father shared, referring to his camp mug. Fond of the memory, he leaned toward me, and rested his forehead on mine. "But that wasn't nearly as fun as this, my darling," he whispered.

I smiled at him, and he smiled back, and we each turned our faces toward the star-scattered night sky.

CHAPTER 9

The next few days passed as usual, but enjoyably enough. Mae and I visited the elephant's waterhole every day, and my mother, having been given school work for us both to do, tutored us; my school work was mailed to us, and Mr. Pang received Mae's school work from her school in their village.

Days rolled by in their own rhythm and Mae and I grew inseparable. It was easy to forget anything could go wrong when every day smelled like wet earth and papayas. But trouble never announces itself — it creeps in quietly, like fog in the hills.

One morning, I woke with an irritatingly painful sore throat and a runny nose. My runny nose tickled, and made me sneeze. Not having to guess what the matter was, I felt my forehead. A mild temperature. Nothing more. The first and most annoying symptom of the common cold is always a sore throat and runny nose. I plunged my hand under my pillow, searching for my handkerchief. It was one my mother had embroidered for me, with my initials and my favourite flower, the waterlily, stitched lovingly in a corner.

I blew my nose, which seemed simultaneously to block it and make me sneeze again. Now, my throat throbbed in agony. It was intolerable. I was burning up beneath my bedclothes so I tossed off the coverlet and got out of bed. At least I could still walk, I thought, as I exited the tent for some fresh air.

My father, as usual, was busy at his typewriter. It seemed that he was suffering from the same complaint, too. So, with that, our adventure came to a temporary halt.

My father and I, the invalids, and stubbornly unhappy to be so, bunked together, neither of us willing to share our illness with anyone but each other, and each took turns to nurse the other.

We passed our days in isolation playing draughts and cards. But it was my father's new cough that was troubling. Sometimes when he coughed, he couldn't catch his breath, and only the vapors of camphor oil that my mother prepared for him would help.

When we were pretty sure we were no longer infectious, though still struggling with our symptoms, we had started to get better, and so, we were allowed visits from Mae and the others.

It was a week before we both recovered – more or less. To my surprise, my father bounced back quicker than I did. My nose remained stubbornly blocked, leaving me with a lingering, chesty cough.

Dr. Banks, who had attended to my mother when she miscarried, diagnosed me with the flu. I was so offended by this, so in denial and so exhausted by the miserable illness to start with, that I burst into tears, "but I don't WANT to have the flu!" I shrieked, "I want to go swimming with the elephants…", I broke, overcome by an almost nauseating coughing fit.

My mother rolled her eyes. "For goodness' sake, Mags," she soothed, "You can't go swimming now. You'll catch your death."

She bathed my head with a cool flannel. "Now," she said softly, "blow your nose."

The last thing I remember was George gently plunging a syringe full of some liquid I didn't recognise, into my arm. It must have put me to sleep, because my eyelids grew heavy, and everything around me went dark.

Fever dreams are strange things. I dreamt I was floating in the elephants' waterhole. The elephants were gathered at the water's edge, shuffling their enormous feet uneasily, making the ground rumble, trumpeting as if concerned for my safety.

I felt a dead weight on my chest, as one does, knowing something bad was looming. I rolled over in the water and started swimming, away from something, I thought. Then all of a sudden, I was staring into the face of a gigantic boa constrictor who flicked his strange, rainbow tongue at me, and fixed his horrible, tallow-eyed stare upon me.

I woke myself with spluttering and started to shiver, whether from worsening fever or terror, I wasn't sure. Then I burst into hiccupping, pitiful wailing.

My parents hurried into the tent. My mother gathered me in her arms and spoke softly to me. My father stood close by, his watchful, loving gaze upon us.

I drifted in and out of sleep, days melting into each other. When I was awake, someone was always near—my father reading quietly, my mother humming while folding laundry, Mae peeking into the tent with worried eyes. Slowly, the heat of my fever began to lift and after a week, I was feeling much better. My father, however, seemed to relapse. One morning, he woke up struggling to breathe. The doctor came, and I waited outside the tent while he visited with my father. I heard Dr. Banks murmuring to my parents, and their replies seemed to indicate their understanding of this 'unfortunate situation,' as Dr Banks called it.

My mother made a distressing sound from deep in her gut, and my father soothed her. I could hear a muffled sort of thumping. It was my mother, beating my father's chest to vent her anger.

"How could you be so stupid?!" she screamed, *"How could you ignore this, you stupid, stupid, stupid man, how could you let*

yourself get so sick?!"

"We knew this already," he said in a hushed, reassuring tone, "This just confirms it, my darling."

The doctor came back the next day carrying a strange contraption. I had never seen anything of its kind before; it was cylinder-shaped, and I thought it looked like a missile from the war I had seen once in a movie.

"What is that?" I asked my mother, eyeing it with suspicion over breakfast.

My mother stared blankly at me. "It's an oxygen tank," she explained, raising her eyebrows matter-of-factly, "for your father's cough."

That's all she told me, but then again, I didn't ask too many questions. I knew I would only be told not to ask about things I wouldn't understand.

The days that followed were quiet—soft and slow, as though the world itself was holding its breath. I couldn't shake the weight in my chest, though I wasn't sure if it came from sadness, or worry, or something else I didn't yet have a name for.

One morning, Mae and I were playing by the waterhole. I wasn't really playing, though—just going through the motions. Mae watched me carefully. She knew me well enough by now to ask,

"What is wrong, Maggies?"

I didn't answer right away. I was staring at the water, watching a dragonfly skim across the surface. Finally, I asked,

"How did your mother die?"

Mae's face changed. She looked down at her feet.

"I not sure," she said softly. "One day, she sick. Next day, she not come back home."

"Did you ask your Pa what happened?"

She shook her head.

Later that day, I heard my parents whispering in my father's part of the tent, his study.

"I want to tell her today," my father insisted.

"Are you sure?" There was a brief silence. Then my mother sighed heavily and said, "There'll never be a *right* time, I suppose. I think she deserves to know. Evelyn..."

Something beyond my control pushed me to open the tent. "Daddy?"

I stood staring at my parents, and I had a horrible feeling the tent had locked itself, even though I knew it couldn't, and it was too late to turn back.

"Hello Mags," my father said warmly, and opened his arms, "Come here for a moment, would you, my love?"

It was cancer, they said. A tumour in his chest. But it

wasn't serious. Radiotherapy, whatever that was, would slow it down, and they, whoever they were, could operate. And they promised emphatically, my father would be just fine.

After he recovered from his attack of illness, which made more sense to me now than it did before I knew about its underlying cause, we returned to Mr. Pang's village. My father had been advised by Dr. Banks that, while the cancer hadn't progressed, he was still too unwell to continue our expedition in the jungle.

Knowing the truth didn't make it any easier to leave. As we packed, I whispered goodbye to the orangutans, to the elephants, to the air that smelled like wildflowers and rain. Then I climbed into the Range Rover, and we drove away.

On the journey back to the village, Mr. Pang thought it would be best to warn us what to expect from his mother, Sun Pang, who, until now, he had neglected to tell us he and Mae lived with.

She was a fiery woman, by the sounds of it, and Mr. Pang had had many smacks with the head of a wooden spoon when he was a boy. He warned that she didn't have much of a grasp of the English language, or British manners. We all laughed. My father's laugh was a sound that had always been quite life-affirming, but so often nowadays, whenever he laughed, it seemed to leave him winded. He coughed, and for the first time, I saw tiny spots of blood on his handkerchief.

Sun Pang, affectionately called Sunny, was a typical mother and grandmother. I think every grandmother must be the same, no matter where on Earth they come from.

She met us at the front door. She was short and slightly round, with tight curls of blackish grey hair secured in a neat bun and fastened to her head by a pretty wooden comb in the shape of the frangipani flower. The sarong she wore was painted with a marine life scene: blue fish, rainbow-coloured fish, and orange starfish in a sparkling ocean.

"*Pang!*" Mrs. Sunny demanded, storming up the path, "Pang, where To?"

Mae, as ever, translated the short exchange for me, and we both giggled at her grandmother's theatrical overexaggeration.

Mr. Pang explained that Mr. To was still recovering from his accident. He said it was Mr. Evelyn, that he needed to look after now.

My father pulled himself heavily up and out of the Range Rover, and my mother took his arm, helping him the rest of the way down.

He looked older than his 35 years. The rigour of his relapse had weakened him, and now he used a crutch to stay on his feet. Nonetheless, he smiled graciously at Mr. Pang's mother and greeted her with his hands in prayer as is customary in Thailand.

"You look like dung, Mr. Evelyn," said Mrs. Sunny, to the horror of her son and surprise of the rest of us, the gaps in her sentence telling of her little understanding of conversational English.

Mae repeated her grandmother's words to me in whispers, hiding her mouth behind her hand, and Mr. Pang scolded her in Malay and gave her a gentle clip around the ear.

"Mama," hissed Mr. Pang, in Malay (this time, Mae did not translate). "You cannot use that word. These people are British. You must try to be polite."

Mrs. Pang looked at Mr. Pang accusingly, clearly offended at being told how to speak.

"Okay," she said, raking my father with motherly concern, "All you, come in. I make you hot drink and spicy soup, Mr. Evelyn. Good to put hairs on your chest!" She spoke enthusiastically and patted my father on the shoulder as she passed us to go inside.

My father had his dinner in bed as my mother became his nurse, and neither spoke, barely a word, between them.

I shared Mae's bedroom. But I couldn't sleep. I had an odd, niggling feeling that Mae and I would be separated. What if we never see each other again? I thought. But, I supposed, only time would tell.

The next morning, when Mae and I were playing hopscotch in the narrow street that separated the Pang family from their neighbours, my mother came out of the house to speak to us and by the look on her face, I immediately assumed the worst. She bent down in front of me, took my hands and said, "Darling… I'm afraid," the words seemed to catch in her throat, but she battled on, "I'm afraid that we have to go home, back to England."

Back to England. I didn't know if a feeling beyond heartbreak existed, but if it did, I felt it now. Despite the sunshine and warmth, I felt the sky go black and the temperature drop, and I was sure it had started to rain. Mae had been my best and only friend since the moment I met her, and now we faced being separated, perhaps forever. My mother gathered me in her arms and spoke softly, doing her best to soothe me. I wept bitterly.

As much as I hated the idea of returning to England, more than anything on Earth, I wanted my father to be healthy. I wanted to continue on adventures with him until he was too old to leave the house, let alone travel the world.

So, with heavy hearts, in the coming days, we travelled to Singapore, where our adventure had begun, and took the long ferry ride back to the London docks.

PART 2

BARKINGS, ENGLAND

CHAPTER 10

While my father recovered from his operation, which was done one week after we returned to England, my mother arranged to send me away for schooling in London. She also took charge of my father's care, which I understood was the right thing to do.

I wish I could say I fondly remembered my time at boarding school. But that would be dishonest. My mother had attended the same school when she was a girl. The school mistress, Miss Cardew, remembered my mother fondly when they spoke on the telephone about a placement for me.

On my departure for school, I bid my father farewell. He was sitting up in bed and, as ever, writing, this time in a journal.

"Not to worry, my love," he said, lovingly patting my hand, "You've got my adventurer's spirit. Don't I always say that? If you can trek the mountains of Burma, you can face the wild animals of boarding school."

His voice still grated slightly, as the operation had taken its toll on his intrepid spirit and tired him. But still, he smiled.

"You'll write to me, won't you?" he said, the smile in his voice adopting a note of hopeful insistence.

Yes, I promised him, *of course I would.*

My mother and I had only a short bus journey as the school was near the city's outskirts. Already unused to the number of layers one had to wear to be comfortable in London, I was utterly stifling in my blue coat, woollen dress, winter stockings, gloves, scarf and hat. My mother, having grown less accustomed to the miserable British climate, was battling a runny nose.

"I think you'll like Barkings, Mags," she chirped.

Barkings, I thought, what sort of stupid name for a school is Barkings?

Miss Cardew, the headmistress, had been the French teacher when my mother attended Barkings. She was a kind lady, my mother told me, who, in actuality, couldn't speak a word of French, and was once caught flicking through the French Language book she kept hidden in her desk drawer; it was a book she kept only for teaching, and she didn't care about France or the language at all.

Barkings was established as a private home in the days of Queen Victoria. It was then bought by nuns shortly after the Queen's death and was a simple nunnery before the Sisters decided to turn it into a school for children orphaned by WWI. It was made of red bricks, with double doors of viridian green, and a surrounding hedgerow on the neatly manicured lawn.

My mother and I walked hand in hand up the front steps of the Barkings' threshold. On the grand entrance doors was an enormous, ancient doorbell of rusty brass polished to within an inch of its life. As we approached, and just before the bell rang, my mother paused, blew her nose, and smoothed down my hair, and hers. First impressions are everything, after all.

The door opened with an ominous creak, and a small woman, who I thought looked something between a vulture in her nun's habit and Mrs. Claus, peeped through.

"Yes?"

"Sister Veronica?" My mother breathed in pleasant tones of salutation.

I was surprised when Sister Veronica remembered my mother and welcomed us warmly. She led us down an oddly dark hallway, hung with various paintings depicting the Virgin Mary and baby Jesus, as well as Christ's crucifixion. There was a strange smell of incense, damp carpet, and soot. Sister Veronica explained the history of the building and a general run-down of the school's curriculum and policy as we walked.

Nine o'clock was lights out. No exceptions. That was when the Sisters entered their hours of silence; in this particular school, the punishment for disturbing those hours of silence, was to wash the windows and polish the silver. I was relieved, as I had expected worse.

During lessons, there was absolutely no talking. Talk during lessons would result in no supper, she explained.

"Don't look so frightened, dear," said Sister Veronica, "Your mother was always a good student. I trust the apple didn't fall far from the tree."

That sounded more like a threat to me, and her sickly-sweet smile didn't do much to reassure me otherwise. My mother patted my shoulder softly with one of her gloved hands. The gloves were made of deep, red leather, lined with thick sheep's wool.

"Alright, my love," she said, sounding rushed, "We'll say cheerio now, shall we? Give me a kiss. I'll pass it to Daddy."

I turned my face toward her. For a moment, everything froze. I didn't want her to leave me. Not here. I wasn't ready. I gave her a peck on the cheek; she didn't linger. She, like my father, hated goodbyes.

When Sister Veronica showed my mother the door, she turned, blew me a kiss, and suddenly, she was gone. Like the wind had carried her away. Sister Veronica closed the door. The click of the latch seemed to echo through the foyer. For a moment, everything was quiet. Too quiet, I thought. Then I heard my mother's gentle sobbing on the other side of the closed door, smothered, I think, by my mother's glove. Then, receding footsteps. She was gone.

Sister Veronica slid the latch across the top of the doors. Then she pulled them together with a thud, ensuring they were locked. I blew my nose.

"Come on now," Sister Veronica sympathised, not unkindly, "No silly tears."

She led me down another dark corridor that seemed to stop before it began and merged into a cramped, boxed-in staircase. I heard the echoes of other children whispering, all seeming too frightened to make a sound. Someone coughed. Then another cough. It was almost as if it came from the plumbing.

A girl sneezed. Someone said, "Bless you," in quite a way that made the girl giggle; that made me smile, but I was too afraid to let Sister Veronica see. They could have been ghosts, for all I knew.

The damp stench made my nose prickle as we crossed the gallery. Sister Veronica took out a large keyring, and inserted it to open a door in front of us. The dormitory was empty.

"Everyone is at Bible studies," Sister Veronica said, "I will give you ten minutes to settle in."

The classroom for Bible studies was across the hall, "The opposite direction to where we came," Sister emphasised, "I suggest you change out of your travelling clothes. You will find a simple frock and pinafore under your pillow. Put them on and join your classmates. *Don't* dawdle."

Sister Veronica rounded on me, looking considerably more like Baba Yaga now than Mrs. Claus, "If you have a cold, you understand you will not be allowed to attend class?" She had picked up on my sniffles.

"It's the damp," I said defensively.

"Don't answer back," she retorted sharply, her voice carrying ominously across the way. She then turned, rather abruptly and the primitive lantern she held disappeared behind her black habit.

The room temperature seemed to drop by several degrees. I sniffed heavily, the smell of damp invading my nostrils, making them heavy. The room was suddenly freezing. I looked around and could see the damp on the ceiling. The pipe in the corner was surrounded by mould, and water droplets were visible on the bends. Beneath it was a large silver pail, filling with the pipes' dripping contents.

I crept over to the pail and looked in. I could see my reflection in the water, which was almost at high tide. I wrapped my arms around myself and shivered. The journey here had not been worth this, I reflected. I closed my eyes and whispered, *Think of the elephants. Think of Mr. Pang and Mr. To. Think of George… Think of Mae.*

There was a quick footfall on the landing. My eyes

cracked open. Then, a girl, around my age, burst in. She stopped in the doorway, her surprise at my presence obvious.

"Hello."

"Hello," I replied.

"You-you must be Margaret…", she said nervously.

"How did you know?" I said, in a tone I can't explain.

"M-Miss Cardew told us to expect you."

She didn't look very well. But then, I thought, somewhat bitterly, who did look very well in England?

"M-m-my n-name's Jane," she seemed to have a stutter.

"Hello," I said.

Jane made a face and fumbled in her pinafore. She took out a filthy white handkerchief that was now grey from overuse. She sneezed rather painfully, "I'm sorry," she said, eyes puffing horribly. She sniffled heavily, "I-I'm not well."

I made a face of my own. I was horrified that it was a face of disgust.

"I can tell," I said kindly, "I'm sorry. It's not nice being ill, is it?"

Jane sneezed again and coughed. Then she blew her nose.

"Sister Veronica doesn't listen when we tell her about the damp," she explained, "Some of the older children have tried to get her to sort it out, but s-she tells us not to, to inter-

inter…"

She sneezed again. I rolled my eyes, but sympathetically, and approached to offer her my handkerchief.

"Here."

"Oh, no, I-I-couldn't."

I huffed, "It's no good using the same one repeatedly. You need a clean one. Please."

Jane raked me with her eyes. Then, carefully, she accepted my gift.

"Th-thank you."

"Now," I said, sounding like my mother suddenly, "blow your nose."

Jane obeyed. She coughed a little and smiled gratefully.

"Which one's your bed?" I asked, looking around.

Jane pointed over my shoulder. The head was directly under an open window, with the foot of the bed facing the plumbing where the damp was. No wonder she was so ill.

"Miss Cardew said you lived in B-B-Burma," Jane said excitedly, her nose heavily congested.

"Well, yes," I said.

"Where is that?" she continued.

I explained that Burma is in Southeast Asia. Jane's eyes lit up, as if she didn't even know there was such a place. My father is a wildlife conservationist, I said. She didn't know what that was. *What on Earth do they teach in this school, then?* I thought.

"It means he helps wild animals. Cleans up their homes and things. Saves them from-from people who want to hurt them."

"Goodness," she said, "that sounds so thrilling."

"Yes," I said. It was all I could say. No words could describe how it felt to travel the world, to make friends with animals you had only read about.

Jane's breath caught in her chest, and she coughed deeply. I thought of my father. I put an arm around her and led her to an empty bed, away from the wretched, damp plumbing and the stupidly open window.

"This isn't my bed," she said anxiously.

"So?"

"*I-we'll* get into t-t-trouble."

"She can try me," I said, challenging Sister Veronica.

I tucked Jane in and fluffed and arranged the pillows. "There," I said, smiling at my new friend.

I looked over my shoulder, crossed the room and closed the open window. I could hear the sound of light traffic. I closed my eyes for a moment, and the sound of car horns, buses and trains became the roar of tigers, the trumpeting of elephants and the calling of monkeys. Jane's loud nose blowing disturbed my thoughts, and I went to sit at the end of her bed.

"I-I don't mean to sound rude," said Jane, unsure how to continue, "but, if you lived so far away, in a lovely warm place, what are you doing *here?*"

"It...", I said, matching her trepidatious tone, "It's complicated."

I explained about my father's illness, and how my mother felt she was doing the right thing by sending me there, and that I agreed with her.

Suddenly, footsteps sounded on the landing. The door opened. Someone gasped — horrified fury.

"Jane Lewis!" said a voice, older than us, but not Miss Cardew or Sister Veronica, "What do you think you're doing in my bed? You filthy little germ-infested slut!"

Jane gasped. She stammered wordlessly and collapsed in a fit of coughing. I stood up, fixing a furious, wide-eyed stare at the looming shadow of a tall girl who had come stomping toward us. She grabbed Jane by the strap of her pinafore.

"How many times have I told you?" she snarled, "You've already covered me with your disgusting snot once today. If I feel so much as the slightest sniffle in the morning, I will make you wish you'd never been born! You know Sister Veronica punishes us for spreading germs. What will she say when I tell her you were in my bed?"

"STOP IT!" I roared, surprising us all. I clapped my

hands over my mouth.

"Who are *you?*" The tall girl said, now shifting her attention to me.

"Never mind *that,*" I retorted, "Who do *you* think *you* are? Shrieking like a banshee at a girl half your size and poorly. You horrible, nasty bitch."

I started backwards with surprise. I had only ever heard the word 'bitch' once when two young women argued on a London street, but I knew it was nasty and should never be used by nice girls like me.

The girl cocked her head, sized me up and cackled like a witch. I was much shorter than she was. She marched up, stared at me as if to challenge me, and slapped me across the face. She probably expected me to fall to the floor, but I didn't. I set my chin but didn't hit her back.

"I hope she does make you ill," I said, carelessly, "At least that would teach you some manners."

She grabbed me by the collar.

"Listen here, you little urchin, I am the head girl at this school. You'll find I have every right to discipline the rest of you gross little maggots. If I threaten anyone for spreading their germs on my pillow, I have every right. But you don't."

The dormitory fell into silence, thick and heavy like the cold air that crept through the cracks. No one dared say another word. I returned to my bed, my cheek stinging, not from the slap but from everything else. I stared at the ceiling, waiting for the darkness to swallow the shame, the fury, the ache of missing home. Sleep did not come easily that night.

CHAPTER 11

I was woken next morning by Jane's loud, congested moaning. She must have gotten worse overnight. I sat up and rubbed my eyes. An older lady was sitting on the bed beside Jane, comforting her after her violent coughing attack.

"Ah," said the woman, "Good morning, Miss Jones. I'm Miss Cardew."

Miss Cardew looked as kind as she sounded. She had one of those faces; when smiling, her whole face lit up, giving off an angelic, golden orb of light.

"Hello," I said happily.

"Blow," said Miss Cardew to Jane, offering her a clean handkerchief.

Jane obeyed. The force of the blowing made her cough a little.

"You'd best be careful, my love," Miss Cardew warned me, kindly, "I'm afraid there's an awful lot of this. Lots of the girls are down with it."

"It's awfully damp," Miss Cardew apologised, "But

Sister Veronica insists we use the funds in more charitably; it's been tough for so many people after the war."

So. Sister Veronica must think she's headmistress, I said inwardly, think again.

Morning light spilled through the dormitory windows, soft but cold. The quiet murmur of girls getting ready filled the air. Jane had drifted off again, her breathing shallow and raspy. I dressed quietly, trying not to wake her, feeling older somehow than I had the day before.

As I ascended the stairs on my way to breakfast, along with the chinking of cups, saucers and cutlery, I heard many unfortunate girls, all simultaneously displaying symptoms they shared with Jane, trying their best to conceal it.

"Harriet!" hissed Sister Veronica, "Cover your mouth, for pity's sake."

That's odd, I pondered, I thought Sister Veronica wouldn't let any sick people to breakfast. I tiptoed into the breakfast room. Miss Cardew rose to her feet, smiling warmly.

"Come in, Miss Jones," she said, "Join us."

I looked around the room. The only vacant seat was beside the tall girl, who I thought would eat me alive. She fixed me with a dangerous glare.

"Elizabeth," warned Miss Cardew, "Do unto others…"

Elizabeth.

Elizabeth rolled her eyes away from me and shuffled in her chair as if making room, giving herself a wide berth. A girl across from us sneezed. Then, looking disgustedly at her hands, she wiped them on her apron.

"*Violet!*" snapped Sister Veronica, "Handkerchief!"

I sat down. With all the sickness around me, I felt like I was inside a Jane Eyre novel. Suddenly, as if from a secret signal I was yet to learn, everyone clasped their hands together and bowed their heads in prayer. I decided to follow.

"For what we are about to receive, may the Lord make us truly thankful," the voice of Sister Veronica declared.

Breakfast was porridge. Well, it was trying to be porridge. It was grey and lumpy, and I couldn't tell if it was made with real oats. I watched a girl across from me take a spoonful, gag and splutter it into her hand. The girl beside her patted her on the back.

"Eat it," hissed Elizabeth, looking dangerously down her nose at me, clearly seeing my disinclination to touch my breakfast, "It's all we get till supper."

When breakfast was over, we filed out without speaking, spoons clinking into empty bowls like bells tolling for the sick. The hallway was just as damp, the air just as bitter, but the thought of fresh air—even cold, grey English air—was a relief.

Many of the girls, at least 15, stayed inside due to illness. I'll be next, I thought, sorry for all the poor, sickly girls inside.

As I panned my new surroundings and the world outside the breakfast hall, I noticed how little colour there seemed to be in England compared to Burma. My imagination took me back to the lush green surrounding the elephant's waterhole; the elephants were drinking from their sweet, clean pool, and blew their trumpeting trunks happily, spraying themselves with water. I could hear the monkeys singing in the trees, the tigers roaring.

"Miss Jones?" Sister Veronica's voice called.

The Burmese jungle began to crack like breaking glass. Then it shattered, and I was back in the dank, cold playground. Sister Veronica loomed over me. "It's time for morning prayers."

Morning prayers were held in the chapel. The chapel seemed small, but surprisingly accommodated all the girls. It had a stained-glass window at the altar, and shuttered windows on either side. Prayers, like everything else at Barkings, were a silent affair. I wondered if this was a Quaker establishment, or did the Sisters just value their silence that much? But no, the place's relics told me this was very much a Catholic school.

With my hands in prayer and eyes closed as if in prayer, I willed myself back to Burma or Africa. Anywhere but here.

"Please," I whispered, "Please take me back. Take me away from England," and, for effect, I added, "Amen."

After prayers, we were all allowed to write letters home. We did this in class and, once again, in silence. Miss Cardew was helping Jane write to her parents. Jane couldn't read or write very well, and was still quite poorly. I noticed Elizabeth was sitting in the corner of the room, reading a book. Perhaps she had no family, or, I supposed, it was possible her family didn't like her very much.

I had been looking forward to writing to my parents since I arrived. But now that I could, I couldn't find the words to write.

Dear Mummy and Daddy…

I scribbled at last…

I hope you are both well (especially Daddy). I am quite fine, but I miss you both terribly, already. It's so cold here, and almost all the girls are ill. I have made a friend, though, I think. Her name is Jane…

As it was only the morning after my arrival, I had little to say beyond those first lines and a short recount of Maths, Science and Bible Studies. I folded my letter and slid it into the outbox. I glanced over at Jane, still pale and the same handkerchief crumpled in her hand. Something in me pulled toward her. Stories, I thought, might help more than soup.

That evening, as the sky darkened outside and the cold crept into our bones, we returned to the dormitory. The scent of eucalyptus and menthol clung to the air, and the hush of girls trying not to cough filled the space between the rustling of blankets.

"Jane?" I said quietly.

"Oh," Jane replied weakly, "Margaret…"

"You can call me Maggie," I said kindly, "Everyone else does."

Jane smiled and closed her eyes for a moment.

"Tell me more about the jungle."

I stopped, a little surprised. I didn't know where to begin.

"Well…", I said, as I sat down beside her.

I told her about Mr. Pang and Mr. To and Mae and how the baby orangutan jumped into my father's arms. Jane's face brightened and, for a moment, she looked much better. I told her about my feverish nightmare and the terrifying rainbow serpent.

The door opened, and we both started at the sound of an explosive sneeze. Miss Cardew came in and ushered Elizabeth, wrapped in a shawl and clutching a handkerchief. Miss Cardew drew back the bedclothes, and Elizabeth climbed heavily into bed. Elizabeth fixed Jane with a stare that would turn the softest beings into stone. She coughed badly, and

Miss Cardew said that she would come back with the "tonic."

"What are *you* looking at?" Elizabeth snarled, glaring at me.

"Well," I said, rather carelessly, "It's not as if you didn't deserve it."

Elizabeth coughed and blew her nose. Jane glanced sideways at me. We smiled at each other with quiet amusement. Justice was sweet.

Days went by, and Jane began feeling better. It was nice to see her in full health. We sat together in class and played together in the playground. We found we had much in common. Her father, she said, was a Geography teacher at the University of Cambridge. Her mother was expecting a baby, and so Jane was sent to boarding school. I thought having a baby was a strange excuse for sending one's daughter away for schooling.

"It's alright," Jane said, shrugging, "It's not for me to say that I want to be at home."

I thought that was a sage thing to say, for a ten-year-old. *Yes*, I thought. *Jane and I are going to be good friends.*

The week rolled by in chilly silence and sniffling coughs. Then came the day of the doctor's visit, which stirred the place like a stone dropped in still water.

He was tall, with greyish brown hair, glasses, and a kind expression that you'd expect from a doctor. Jane and I hid behind the door of our dormitory to watch Dr. Hancock examine Elizabeth. He was peering critically down his nose at her, his fingers tenderly investigating her lymph nodes.

"*Hmmm...*" he droned, and put the earpieces of his stethoscope in his ears.

Sister Veronica and Miss Cardew stood by Elizabeth's bed, waiting to hear his diagnosis. Elizabeth looked up from under her eyelids at Dr. Hancock.

"Well. For a start," began the doctor, "I would very much like to know how you managed to imitate the symptoms you claim to be suffering, Miss Bellamy."

Elizabeth's eyes grew wide with offence.

"What?" said the horrified Sister Veronica.

"How dare you!" said Elizabeth, eyes narrowed threateningly at Dr. Hancock, "It's that little rat Jane that gave me her germs, I..."

"Elizabeth," Miss Cardew interrupted, "Be quiet this instant."

Elizabeth crossed her arms and sniffed heavily. I could see now that it was more a sniff of complete disapproval than anything else. Sister Veronica marched up to Jane and felt her forehead.

"There's *nothing* wrong with you, you stupid, wicked

girl. Get up! Get out of bed this instant!" she bellowed.

"But…" Elizabeth contested.

Sister Veronica pulled Elizabeth forcefully from her bed.

"Now, Sister…" said Miss Cardew with calm, level-headedness.

Sister Veronica took the leather belt from around her waist with remarkable agility. She dealt Elizabeth's rear with lash after lash. The more Elizabeth screamed, the further Sister thrashed. I noticed a terrifying twinkle in the Sister's eyes, wide with enjoyment, glowing a strange yellow and her tongue poking out slightly between clenched teeth.

That night, I couldn't stop hearing the belt. The sound of leather on skin echoed long after it stopped. No one spoke about it. We all just stared down into our porridge bowls and the damp-stained ceilings, pretending nothing had happened. But children are never truly silent. Not in their thoughts.

"She's a *werewolf*!" Jane whispered to me when we had gone to bed that night.

We had secretly pushed our beds closer together at some point during the day, but were now sharing my bed, each hiding from the outside world under a patchwork tent. I taught her to make shadow puppets with the light from my candle. I did my best to tell her the story of our trek up the mountain using shadows, but orangutans were difficult to replicate with my hands.

It was nice to see my innocent little friend's face brighten. Somehow, though, it reminded me just how much I missed Mae.

CHAPTER 12

The next morning, a letter came. We were at breakfast when Miss Cardew handed it to me. I almost choked with the shock and surprise at receiving a letter. It was from my father.

Dear darling Mags, it said, *it made me so happy to hear you are alright. I know it will be different for you, but I promise it won't be for long. I am feeling much better. I still have a sore throat, and the doctor says it will be painful for a while, but other than that, I'm fighting fit.*

My Mags, I care more about you than myself and am counting the days until we'll be together again. It won't be long.

I want to take you to Africa. Africa, my darling! Think of that; the place is alive with all the animals you've only seen in books.

Your mother has been a marvellous nurse. I owe it all to her that I have recovered so well. And to you, my sweet Mags; it's the thought of seeing you that has been the light at the end of this long tunnel, and while your mother has given me all the care and medicine, I only have to think of you and I am almost cured (that's just between us. I don't want to hurt Mummy's feelings so, Shhhh).

You know I love you both with equal madness.

    Yours, Daddy.

The next morning, Elizabeth wasn't in class, so, after classes ended for the day, I went down the long hallway searching for her. The hallway, dimly lit and freezing cold at the best of times, felt particularly dark and cold that day. I opened one door after another as I went, thinking she could be hiding.

"Elizabeth?" I called into the darkness. "Elizabeth?" My voice made an eerie echo. Then, the far-off sound of someone being sick, violently sick and the sound of a strange cry, unlike any other I had heard before. Elizabeth. I ran, shuffling my feet toward the sound. I could just make out the shine of something wet in the lantern light - a pool of vomit on the floor.

I strained to see the shadow of something up ahead. It was Elizabeth, bent over a statue of the Virgin Mary. When each vomit subsided, she clung to the statue, sobbing.

"Elizabeth?"

"Go away!" she pleaded through sobs.

"Are you alright?"

There was a gagging cough in the dark, as if Elizabeth was repulsed by her own sickness. She emerged with a letter in her hand, her face tear-stained and drained of all colour.

"What are you staring at?" she demanded.

"I just wanted to see if you were alright," I said defensively.

Elizabeth burst into tears. The note in her hand floated to the floor. I was torn between wanting to comfort her and wanting to stay put; for some reason, I couldn't ignore her earlier cruelty. I tiptoed toward her and bent to pick up the note. It took all I had to stop my hand from shaking. I glanced at the hasty scribble.

"Oh!" I gasped.

Elizabeth sniffled.

"She-she died just after I got here," Elizabeth explained, her voice shaking, "my-my poor baby sister!"

She burst into wailing. The letter dropped out of my hands as I stared blankly at Elizabeth.

"I'm sorry," I said, my voice quivering with sadness.

Elizabeth wiped her nose with the sleeve of her cardigan. "What would you know?" she said bitterly.

I started with surprise. What would she know about what I knew about sadness? Stop it, said my conscience sternly, *remember how lucky you are. You have no right to judge.*

Elizabeth slid down the wall, burying her face in folded arms on her knees. I went to sit beside her. I knew better than to touch her, so I slid a little closer and lowered myself beside her. I wanted her to know she wasn't alone.

"Why did you pretend to be ill?" I said.

I knew at once that it was wrong, but I had to say something, if only to distract Elizabeth from her grief.

"I don't know," she croaked, full of emotion, "I don't like Jane, I suppose. I never have."

"Why not?" I asked.

Elizabeth shrugged. Full tears rolled down her cheeks. Desperately, I patted the front of my pinafore. Then remembered I had given my hanky to Jane.

I supposed I couldn't tell her what I knew about sadness. At least my father was alright. Elizabeth's mother had lost a child. My problem paled in comparison.

"I'm sorry," said Elizabeth, "that I was awful to you when-when we first met."

I shrugged. "That's alright."

Elizabeth made a face, "But, if you tell anyone that you almost stepped in my sick, I'll flush you down the lav. Do you understand?"

I smiled at that, disguising it by wiping my mouth with my apron.

CHAPTER 13

The next day, a man arrived at Barkings to fix the plumbing. We girls all gathered out of curiosity at the end of the hall. He was a short, fat man in dirty overalls and a peaked cap. His middle wobbled as he got heavily down on his knees, armed with a spanner. He gave the plumbing a loud *whack*. There was a strange groaning, and a gurgle, like a growling stomach.

"There!" said the man in a thick, cockney accent, "Good as new!"

"I do hope you're not expecting payment, Mr. Williams," Sister Veronica purred, "because, not only have 10 of our girls been down with colds since that wretched pipe started making the dormitory damp, but ever since then we have been trying to get your lot out here to fix it, *THIS DAMN PLUMBING!*"

So great was the force of Sister Veronica's anger that the plumber gave a little jump. She must have surprised herself with her own outburst as she crossed herself and whispered, *"Hail Mary, full of grace, the Lord is with thee. Blessed art thou among women and blessed is the fruit of thy womb, Jesus."*

The gathering of girls at the end of the hall giggled. Then, a sharp look from Miss Cardew. I caught Elizabeth in the corner of my eye, she was smiling, her cheeks rosy with delight. At least she had forgotten to be sad.

After chapel and morning prayer the following Sunday, it began to rain. It came down in sheets and, while I could close my eyes and remember rainy days in the Burmese rainforest, something about the English rain was more miserable. It was as though the English sky was so used to the rain that it sighed and made it cold.

Despite the rain, Sister Veronica insisted on continuing with our routine Sunday morning walks. She walked briskly, and insisted we kept up. In pairs, as instructed, I walked with Jane, and although she was my age, she was quite small, so I had to hold her hand so she didn't get left behind.

Sister walked us through puddles, so the water seeped through my boots, saturating my socks. I worried for poor little Jane, having just recovered from a violent illness, now trudging through driving rain.

We walked through Kensington Gardens where the statue of Peter Pan had stood since 1912, and even he, in all his bronze glory, was sodden with rain.

Through the pounding rain, I heard some of the girls splutter and sneeze. As I often did in England with its weather,

I closed my eyes momentarily. I returned to the memories of the humid rainforests of Burma, but it didn't help to warm me up.

We all raced to take off our many layers when we arrived back at Barkings. The wooden floor beneath us was wet from our boots and the rain on our coats. Still, at least the plumbing was fixed so we all looked forward to warm baths.

In the bath, I hugged my knees and shivered; the water was barely up to my waist. Suddenly, Sister Veronica threw a pale of cold water over my head. Its icy nature made my breath catch in my throat each time I breathed in.

"Cold baths are healthy," Sister said briskly, as she took a scrubbing brush and proceeded to scrub my hair.

"Says *who*?" I murmured in a trembling whisper of disbelief.

She didn't answer. Soap in my eyes, I rubbed them and listened to her footsteps suddenly recede. I sat shivering. Then, when she returned, she threw another bucket of cold water over me. I coughed.

After bathing, it was time for Bible studies. I couldn't seem to get warm, and at the same time, I was sweating profusely from under my linen dress and thick winter pinafore. I breathed in, and my chest rattled like train tracks under a train.

"Miss Jones!" snapped Sister Veronica, "quiet that cough!"

"Yes, Sister." I said, desperately. Then I sneezed into my apron, and some girls gasped in disgusted horror that I had dirtied my uniform.

"Shut up!" Elizabeth shouted.

"*ELIZABETH!*" shrieked Sister Veronica.

I felt Jane's arm wrap around me as a coughing fit assaulted me, and Elizabeth came and swept a hand over my forehead.

"Sister!" she cried, "Sister, she's burning up."

Suddenly, there was chaos and noise as the whole class panicked. Everyone crowded me, and the heat of their bodies made my head spin. I felt dizzy. A black shadow grew before me, and then someone caught me. Then, nothing.

Later, I woke shivering in a chair by a dormitory window. The blanket wrapped around me was warm, but scratchy, more uncomfortable than comfortable. I felt tired, so closed my eyes again. The jungle appeared, as it always did when I needed it most, but it seemed distorted and far away, as though I was under water, sinking fast.

"Where is Miss Jones?" came a voice, returning me slightly to consciousness.

"She's got the shakes," said Violet.

"Should we see if she's alright?" said Elizabeth.

My head grew heavier. Everything went black. There was no jungle, no waterhole, no elephants. Occasionally, my eyes cracked open, and I noticed Miss Cardew bathing my forehead. I was hot and cold by turns. Then, nothing.

I don't know how long I was asleep, but when I woke, the sun was beaming through the window, and Elizabeth stood over me, cooling my brow with a damp cloth. Jane was by my side, leaning forward, chin in hands as if she'd been waiting for me to wake for days.

"What are you two doing here?" I suddenly croaked, surprising myself.

I had been asleep for almost five days, Elizabeth explained. The doctor came. Pneumonia, he said. Deeply confused, I frowned.

"Miss Cardew told Sister Veronica not to take us on walks in the rain anymore," said Jane, sounding excited by the whole thing.

We laughed. My laughter turned to a gurgling sort of splutter. I blew my nose.

"Dr. Hancock says you must rest for two weeks," said Elizabeth kindly.

"Two weeks?!" I croaked.

"*Shhhh,*" hushed Elizabeth.

I rolled my eyes and threw my head onto my pillow.

"I wouldn't be too upset if I were you," Elizabeth warned with a note of kindness, "Miss Cardew orders all the best things for the invalid girls. You'll have *all* the best food *and* the best bed linen and blankets."

"Sister Veronica just wants to see us all freeze to death," I said bitterly.

"I didn't say anything about Sister Veronica, did I?" Elizabeth pointed out, dipping the cloth into the washbowl, wringing it and touching it to my forehead, "You're lucky that you're being paid any attention at all."

"You're saying all the other sickly girls are lucky?" I said doubtfully, "You think Jane is lucky?"

Elizabeth flicked Jane a look. "She's lucky she isn't dead," she explained, my attitude irritating her now, "you both are."

Resting for two weeks was very dull. Some of the girls from my dormitory gave me books to read, none of which I was invested enough to finish, and so I started to read many of them at once, but was too bored to concentrate and finish any.

While I was now at least awake, I still had aching limbs. This was quite annoying; I was so used to trekking mountains, that the inability to use my legs was depressing.

I wondered how my father was getting on. He, like me,

would hate to have to be idle, and he would have to be idle for much longer than I.

I closed my eyes, once again trying to conjure the Burmese jungle. I lingered for a while in the black of unconsciousness. Then, an expanding kaleidoscope of colour, and I found myself at home. I saw my father lying in bed, my mother beside him, holding his hand. She was softly weeping, and I noticed my father's face had changed, there in body, but not in spirit. He was dead.

I gasped, as one often does on the edge of deep sleep, my body telling me I was still alive. I knew in my heart that it was just a dream; my father was alive. He had to be. But, for some reason, I cried. My friends must have heard me, for Jane, Elizabeth, and other girls hurried over to me.

Without words or fuss, Elizabeth threw her arms around me and stroked my hair, whispering words of comfort to me. I clung to her, feeling the sleeve of her dress soaking with tears.

"I want to go home!" I sobbed, hiccupping with the force of emotion.

By home, I meant I wanted to be back in Burma with my mother and father. I couldn't contain my wailing; I tried, but my chest ached with the effort it required, and as I wept like it was the end of the world, I felt my sadness, which was at full tide waning, and a further attack of heartbroken hiccups came upon me.

I felt Jane fling her birdlike arms around me, and Elizabeth hugged me tighter. Was that a tiny kiss in my hair? Their warmth surged through me like a thick blanket, and the hand on my head was not much bigger than my mother's; if I did not know it was Elizabeth, with my eyes closed, she could have been my mother. I clung to Elizabeth's pinafore front and howled.

"It's alright, Maggie," Elizabeth whispered, "it was just a bad dream."

Her hand swept my head, fingers running gently through my fevered tangle of curls. Jane was whimpering beside me, and I felt my shoulder growing wet with her tears; "Hush, Jane!" someone snapped in the dark.

"No, *you* hush!" Elizabeth retorted softly, "this has nothing to do with any of you. Maggie's upset. Everyone, *go away!*"

I hadn't believed Elizabeth when she told me that she was *head girl of this miserable place*, but when I saw all the other girls scuttle away in fear, I felt a surge of enormous respect for her. My newfound respect seemed to stem the flow of tears and quiet the unyielding sobs, and before I knew it, my head floated into my pillow once again, and I fell asleep. Elizabeth's arms around me unwound themselves, and I felt the quilt go over me and shivered slightly as the warmth spread from my toes to the top of my head.

"Good night, Maggie," Elizabeth whispered, patting my head lightly.

CHAPTER 14

I spent the next week in bed. I used the time quite productively, and started drawing pictures with borrowed pencils and paper from Miss Cardew. I drew the elephants in their waterhole, my father with his little orangutan friend, and the face of my friend, Mae.

Miss Cardew received my paintings graciously, and deemed proud of my artistic flare. She hung them on the wall of the dormitory, which, she said, gave it new light and life.

"You have a wonderful talent, Miss Jones!" she said, breathless with amazement. "You must have had a good tutor in Burma?"

"Yes," I replied, shyly, "It was my mother."

"Well," Miss Cardew said, smiling brightly, "I'm sure your parents are very proud of you."

"Today is a special day, Miss Jones," Miss Cardew said as she led me to her office after breakfast soon after I had fully recovered. She said I was to have a hot bath, contrary to Sister

Veronica's disinclination to use the hot water, and make sure I looked my absolute best.

Back in the dormitory, Miss Cardew ran the bath herself as I selected an outfit from the modest selection of clothing I had brought with me to Barkings. I didn't understand why I was being treated so kindly, but the feeling of warm water on my skin was as close to Heaven as I had been in the almost two months since my arrival. Miss Cardew added a few drops of lavender oil to the bath water, and I breathed it in with a luxuriant sigh.

"Did you pick out your best dress, Maggie?" Elizabeth asked, as she combed my hair while I sat in my towel at the end of my bed.

"Why? … Ow!" I screeched as the comb caught a particularly difficult curl. But by the disapproving look on her face, she had been sworn to secrecy.

"Fine," I said petulantly.

Just as I had patted down the front of my dress in approval, the ancient doorbell chimed down stairs. The same ominous creak of the entrance doors entered my ears. Someone had arrived. Elizabeth and I rushed to the landing to peer over the railing at who it was. We could her the whispers of Miss Cardew and Sister Veronica greeting a man and woman, but we couldn't see them.

Then, I heard the sound I had been waiting two months to hear.

"Mags!?" shouted my father, "Where are you, my love?"

A gasp caught in my throat. If ever anyone had died from happiness, I could have done at that moment. Father's voice was hoarse, but it still sounded like him. He was alive, and he was there! With reckless abandon, I ran down the hallway, flew down the stairs like a shooting star and caught the site of my parents in the doorway, smiling up at me. With open arms, my father swept me off the last two steps and into his arms. He was thinner, much of his muscle wasted from illness, but he looked healthy. I felt his body heave as he sighed, overcome with relief at the site of me. I burst into tears and felt my mother's embrace around us both, rubbing her hand up and down my back as if to erase the months of separation. My father's fingers were tangled in my curls, gripping my head tight as if afraid to let me go. He pulled away only to cover my cheeks in kisses.

"Well, Mr. Jones," Miss Carew interrupted warmly, "I'm so glad you have recovered."

"Thank you, Miss Cardew," my father replied.

I looked up to see Elizabeth, Jane and the other girls gathered on the landing, all of them smiling down on us.

Later, with my bags packed, I prepared to farewell my

Barkings friends. It was strange to think that I would never return, and may never see Jane or Elizabeth again. Although it was a rocky start, Elizabeth and I had become something like friends and I had grown fond of her comfort.

It was Jane I would miss. She was the last to bid me farewell.

"Don't worry," I said cheerfully, "We'll see each other again, I know we will."

Jane hugged me tight and whimpered softly into my shirt, leaving a small wet patch near my belly button.

My father crouched down by Jane with his elbow on his knee. His mouth flickered into a smile as he said, "May I give you something, Jane, is it?"

Jane hiccupped, and through sniffles, nodded, "Mm-hm."

My father took a small wooden carving from his trouser pocket. It was an elephant with its trunk in the air.

"Here," he said kindly as he handed her the elephant carving. "I know Mags has told you all about Burma and the elephants. This will make sure you *never* forget her."

He then looked up at me and added, "I know she'll never forget you; that's a promise."

"Thank you," Jane said shyly and graciously.

My father smiled briefly at her and lovingly stroked her cheek.

I smiled. Not that I had been altogether miserable at Barkings, but I was excited to be going to a new country on another adventure. I turned and watched Barkings shrink into the distance as we drove away.

CHAPTER 15

We were going to Africa, where Mr. Pang, Mae and George would meet us in Cape Town.

"I did promise you, didn't I?" my father said fairly, shrugging one shoulder. "Mr. Pang has created quite an enterprise while we've been away, Mags," he added, proud of his friend.

"What's an enterprise?" I asked, confused.

"It means a business, Mags," my mother kindly whispered.

My father explained that Mr. Pang had inherited some money after his grandmother died, not long after I arrived at Barkings. He bought a share in the nature reserve in Burma and hoped to expand to Africa next. I was happy to hear that the Pang family were doing well.

As we approached the London docks, the brackish scent of the water flooded my senses. I licked my lips, tasting the gritty salt that filled the air.

Once settled in our cabin, my father instantly set to work at his typewriter. I had so deeply missed seeing him sitting there, slightly hunched over the keys with a pencil between his teeth, occasionally moving it behind his ear when he knew he wouldn't need it for a while.

Now and then, he looked up from his work and smiled at me. I wondered for the first time since our new adventure began, what he was writing. Surely, he wasn't journalling nothing, I thought to myself.

As he hunched over the typewriter, sleeves rolled to the crook of his elbows, his partially unbuttoned shirt revealed a small, pinkish-white scar on his chest. Catching my glance, my father covered the scar with his hand. I felt his shame and sensed his thoughts; *that's why I sent you to school, to protect you from this.*

It's alright, replied the flicker of a smile I gave him back, *I understand.*

CHAPTER 16

"Ahoy!" came a voice I immediately recognised as George.

Our taxi stopped, and George opened the door for my mother and me; "Well!" he said, "and who is this grown-up young lady before me?! I say, I'd almost forgotten what you looked like, Lady Mags."

I threw my arms around him, and he lifted me out of the cab. Then I heard Mae's voice behind him. She pushed George out of the way and threw her arms around me.

"Maggies!" she exclaimed.

We danced in a circle to the call of seagulls above us.

"Evelyn!" George said, shifting his attention to my parents.

My father greeted George with open arms. "Hello, my friend!"

They embraced and clapped each other heartily on the back.

"It's good to see you, old chap," George said earnestly,

patting my father lightly on the cheek, "and looking so jolly well!"

With pleasantries over, George informed us that we were headed first for Kruger National Park. A man called Mr. Adebayo would take us into the mountains to observe a band of gorillas and their environment. My father was to record his observations and assist George and Mr. Pang with habitat maintenance, as they had done in Burma. Mr. Adebayo would be our guide and protector.

A jeep pulled up beside us, and a friendly-looking man with a round face that reminded me of a Buddha stepped out of the driver's side. He wore a wide-brimmed felt, khaki hat and ranger's uniform. Disconcertingly, I also noticed a huge machete in a scabbard on his belt.

"Hello, Mr. Jones!" belted Mr. Adebayo, "and Mr. Pang and Mr. Ainsworth, I presume?"

'Mr. Ainsworth' was George. Mr. Adebayo spoke perfect English.

With introductions made and London again behind us, we loaded our bags into the jeep and began the long journey north.

The landscape began to change, and so did the mood — quiet, expectant, as if Africa herself were drawing us in. My father, on the other side of recovery, fell asleep shortly after our departure from Cape Town; my mother followed soon after, and I noticed Mr. Pang had also fallen asleep in the passenger seat. Mae and I were wide awake, too excited to even think of sleep.

The jeep swept fresh dust and dry earth into the air. It mingled with the smell of petrol, and just like in Burma, the stench of cattle and chickens filled our nostrils.

We made our way from Cape Town to Limpopo, the gateway into the rest of Africa. Mr. Adebayo lived somewhere in the Western Cape of South Africa, where we were welcome, he said, to rest for the night.

"My wife will look after us well," he said with a smile.

On arrival at Mr. Adebayo's home, his wife and daughter stood in the doorway, waiting to greet us. Mae and I were delighted that Mr. Adebayo's daughter looked around the same age as us and shared her father's generous smile.

Eager to stretch his legs, George jumped out of the jeep, stretched broadly, and stifled a huge yawn.

"Mrs. Adebayo," George said, "How nice to meet you."

Mrs. Adebayo returned the sentiment, and when George turned to the little girl, she went down on bended knee in greeting.

"I say," George started with surprise, "Jolly nice to meet you, too, little one."

The girl smiled and nodded a bow.

Her name was Grace. She wore simple overalls with a colourful t-shirt, and a beautiful, rainbow turban around her head.

"Hello!" exclaimed the ever-confident Mae, "You, Maggies and my friend?"

Grace giggled politely. "Yes," she said.

Mr. Adebayo clapped my father on the back as if he were already an old friend, and ushered us inside.

Mr. and Mrs. Adebayo's house was very cozy, in the best way. It was a large bungalow with a long hallway and white, tiled floors. Beautiful wall-hangings with tigers and monkeys, and tall statues carved like black panthers, guarded the entrance. The aroma of curry wafted through the air. Mrs. Adebayo told us that goat curry was Grace's favourite.

After supper, we all went out onto the terrace. Mrs. Adebayo and my mother drank tea, and Grace was sent to fetch a bottle of whiskey for the men, which she poured expertly.

We girls dove straight into the luxurious, oval swimming pool with a waterfall feature cascading over a rock wall. We didn't have bathing suits, so we swam carefree in our shirts and knickers.

Mae, Grace and I set up beds in the sitting room at bedtime. We made a fort from pillows, cushions and bedclothes, and while Mae and Grace seemed to have a strange ability to sleep where they fell, I remained wide awake.

The sound of monkeys and birds in the distance was quite soothing, but the lions' roar, seemingly near the house, made me uneasy.

Unsure of my motivation, I had an insatiable urge to go and see that the danger wasn't too close by. I crept from the fort's safety and tiptoed across the tiled floor. The folding door to the terrace opened easily enough, so I stepped outside. The cement was cold under my feet, but the warm night air and the foolish thrill of unwittingly putting myself in danger warmed me.

"Hello," I whispered into the darkness, "Is anyone there?"

There was a deep, low growling sound in the not-too-far distance. Desperate, I looked around and grabbed the first thing I saw; the rifle leaning against the wall.

I took aim into the darkness, and without a second thought, I unlocked the gun and fired.

Suddenly, there was panic and chaos as the house woke. I felt myself going into shock, and the noise around me became muffled. A hand snatched the rifle from my grip. I turned to see my mother screaming at me, but I couldn't hear a word. My father twisted away from us all and fired the rifle into the night sky to empty it of ammunition.

"What the hell do you think you were doing!?" my

father bellowed, "You could have killed yourself, or someone else!" His voice broke as he shouted like I had never heard him do before. I felt like I could see his heart breaking a little. His chest was heaving as if it might burst, as he glared at me, eyes dark with fear.

Then, he raised his hand.

"Evelyn, no!" My mother screamed in terror.

She grabbed my father's raised wrist, and they froze for a moment, my father's body rigid with the fury wrought by adrenaline; his hand shaking under my mother's tight grip.

My mother let go and cradled my father's cheeks to soothe him.

"It's alright," she whispered, "She's alright."

My father pursed his lips. His eyes filled with tears, his bottom lip quivered; then he fell to his knees, the gun falling to the floor. I ran into his open arms and we both wept. I felt his large, gentle hands stroking my hair.

"I'm sorry," he murmured, "I'm so sorry."

CHAPTER 17

The breakfast table was silent after the events of the night before.

"She's just young," I heard my mother whisper to my father as they settled into bed after the situation had been handled. "I know you. You would have done the same for your parents, even at that age."

My father breathed a heavy sigh of defeat, "I know I would have," he said, "that's what was so damned terrifying."

Although my parents' whispered words felt like forgiveness, their meaning lingered with me as we prepared to leave the Adebayos' village.

The sun was still low in the east, and a beautiful pinky-purple against the hazy blue of dawn greeted us.

My father and his colleagues were all set to prepare their rifles, pencils, notebooks, and clipboards. My mother and Mrs. Adebayo packed sandwiches in heavy lunchboxes and boiled water to put in the thermos.

The drive ahead was long, and the tension from the night before hung quietly between us. My father reached into his breast pocket – where he usually kept his cigarettes – and pulled out a small cardboard box. Instead of lighting up this time, he took out a toothpick and slipped it between his teeth. He chewed thoughtfully, the toothpick bobbing up and down like a tiny seesaw.

"Mags!" My mother pointed, trying her best to conceal her excitement. "Up there! Do you see it?"

We all saw a brightly coloured hornbill high in a tree, singing with contentment. My mother slid an arm around me and drew me close. She was smiling. I turned to my father because he was the one with whom I usually shared the excitement of seeing new animals, but he seemed distant.

George stood up in the jeep and took a few photos. Mr. Pang pointed to the birds in the trees and their well-built nest, leaning into Mae to share in the excitement.

My father coughed and scratched at the scar on his chest. It looked like it bothered him, but from the inside, somehow. My mother must have noticed too; she turned and swept her gaze over my father's face. He offered a reassuring smile, but it did little to ease my worry.

The jeep took a steep, rocky mountain climb to the top of the dense rainforest and was welcomed by the joyful symphony of monkeys, birds and lions.

"Daddy?" I whispered, tapping him on the shoulder.

He twisted to look at me and flicked a tired smile.

"Daddy… those lions are a long way away, aren't they?"

My father's face brightened as he chuckled softly, "Don't worry, darling. I think we'll be safe."

The air was heavy with moisture as we walked a narrow track surrounded by young trees and old, thick, twisting vines that hung like bunting from the trees. There were families of macaques nestled in some of the trees, some swinging gleefully from vine to vine, and they seemed to call out, greeting us.

The gorillas were all gathered in a vast clearing. At a distance, there looked to be a narrow, winding path, overgrown with green grass tangled in weeds; the little valley was streaked in sunshine, and the gorillas were happily sitting down to a communal meal.

Mae made to open her mouth, no doubt about to shout in excitement, but Mr. Pang silenced her with a swift hand over her mouth.

My father stooped beside me, and I felt his warm hands on my hips. "We must be very quiet, Mags," he whispered. "Do you see the little ones. Just there?"

He pointed to a pair of baby gorillas, and I nodded. They were more impressive, even than the orangutans. I thought that looking at them with their huge heads and massive, broad, powerful backs was to fear them, but in a way that one fears God.

My mother watched the gorillas through a pair of large binoculars - ones my father had given her on their 10th wedding anniversary, just before my 10th birthday. My father looked up at her with a deep love that almost seemed unreal. They lingered there, eyes locked, until he lifted her hand and kissed it. My mother's expression held a mix of concern and quiet gratitude, while something in my father's face tightened, as if he were bracing against a pain no one could see. I didn't understand it then, but the silence between them made me uneasy, like something important was being left unsaid.

Lost in my confusion at their exchange, I stumbled slightly backwards, and something snapped beneath my tread. I gasped, and everyone turned sharply toward me. There was a grunt from behind me. My father, reaching out for me, grabbed my arm and jerked me behind him as the ape rose, slowly and magnificently, to its feet.

"Don't. Move. A muscle." My father said through clenched teeth.

The alpha gorilla snorted and fixed us with a threatening stare. He lowered on all fours and motioned to his family to move out.

My father fell to his knees and gathered me in his arms, and more from shock than pain, I broke into quiet sobbing.

"You're alright, my darling," my father spoke softly into

my hair, "They're gone now. We're alright. I've got you."

I heard a clicking behind us; it was Mr. Adebayo with his rifle. He fired a warning shot, then another to ensure the gorillas didn't return. Frightened by the noise, a cacophony of birds and monkeys rallied around us against the threat.

The cheerful torches lit the camp like street lamps that night - tall wooden poles with a dancing flame licking the night air.

Mae, Grace and I lay beneath the starry sky, staring into the wide-open carpet of twinkling fairy dust long after the adults had retreated to their tents.

"Mae?" I purred curiously, turning my face toward her.

"Yes, Maggies?"

"Do-do you think that, when we die, someone, I mean, do you think that when someone dies, we come back as other things?"

Mae made a face.

"You means rebirth, yes? My father tells me about rebirth. It in Buddhist religion. I believe."

"What do you want to come back as?" I asked her.

"Hmm," Mae began, deep in thought. "I come back cobra snake. Bite people not my friend!"

We all giggled.

I turned to Grace, "What about you, Grace?"

"Huh," said Grace, "I don't know. Maybe a zebra?"

"Why zebra?" a confused Mae asked.

"Because they're fast," Grace replied.

"But not fast like cheetah," Mae added.

"I think I'd like to be an elephant," I said. "Then I'd be so tall I could see from here to France. And elephants are meant to have good memories, so I'd never forget anything. Not the important things, anyway." I concluded fairly.

I sat up long after Mae and Grace had gone to bed; something about a campfire hypnotised me, making me stare into its red and orange flames. I listened to the sounds of the jungle, sounds I had become so familiar with that they were almost like white noise; the chirping of crickets, the call of nocturnal birds, the chattering of monkeys, as unready for sleep as I was.

I felt the magic of the place seep into my skin. The effect was like medicine, and I remembered the needle that the doctor had given me at Barkings, but this was different. This medicine was something beyond healing, if there was such a thing.

Suddenly, I was jolted back to reality when I heard a low growling in the darkness, like the sound I had heard when I had taken the rifle and shot it at nothing. Whatever it was out there, it didn't sound like retreating this time. It growled again, and I saw a shape moving, a shadow on the ground. I stumbled to my feet and started backing toward the safety of the tents. Then I saw it. A huge male lion stalked out of the surrounding trees and headed slowly toward me. *Stay still*, I told myself as I closed my eyes, *stay still and stay quiet, whatever happens.*

I felt my chest heave as I became dizzy. I put a hand out.

"Hello," I shakily stuttered. "Don't worry. I'm your friend. Now, please. Don't hurt me."

Then, without warning, the animal gave a short, threatening growl and approached me with increasing speed. I wanted to turn and run, but instinct told me I shouldn't if I wanted to survive. When it had almost closed the gap between us, the lion roared and prepared to pounce. Then, as if sent by angels, a loud trumpeting sounded from a nearby bush, and the rumble of huge feet crashing through it made the big cat cease in its pursuit of me, its prey.

An enormous bull elephant charged straight for the lion and, throwing his trunk in the air, he screamed, lifting a gigantic foot as if it could crush the lion with one stomp. The lion cowered, shrinking to the ground. The elephant gave another ear-splitting trumpet and rose briefly on its hind legs. The lion slunk backwards, keeping its eyes fixed on me, until he disappeared.

"Maggie!" My father's voice echoed into the night.

Three rifles suddenly pointed over my head in the dark, and everyone gathered around me. My mother bent down in front of me and brushed away the hair that clung to my face from the sweat of terror.

"Are you alright?" she pleaded.

I nodded.

"Are you sure?" My mother pressed.

"Yes," I managed, "I think so. Yes."

As suddenly as he appeared, the elephant quietly retreated into the darkness. My saviour disappeared as we all watched in shock and gratitude at the magnificent animal.

My father's chest was heaving. I glanced at him as he took his handkerchief and mopped the perspiration from his face and brow. He gave a breathless cough. *No…* said the little voice inside me. *Please, not again.*

CHAPTER 18

After breakfast, Mr. Adebayo, who had slipped away several times during the meal, disappeared again for a while, this time taking Grace with him. On return, he announced that he had arranged a surprise for us.

"What's going on?" Mae demanded of me, confused, "It's not nice he go, then come back, then go again! Where he go?"

"Beats *me*," I said, shrugging. "Maybe they're throwing a surprise party?"

"What for?"

"I don't know," I said, "just be patient."

"What patient?"

I huffed and dragged Mae away from the campsite for no reason other than to distract her. There was no work today, so finding our own adventure was in order.

"Hey!" Grace shouted after us, "Wait for me!"

"We go find our own elephants!" Mae exclaimed.

"She means we're going to look for elephants," I

translated to Grace.

"But that is dangerous," Grace gasped, "The elephants in Limpopo are not like where Mae is from."

"We'll be alright if we stick together," I said, "Come on!"

We crept past the tents, and I heard the gentle *tap, tap, tap* of my father's typing. I craned my neck in passing and saw my father through the mesh window, bent over his typewriter. There was a storm lantern beside him on his desk, the wick turned down low, bathing the white walls of the tent with beautiful, shy golden candlelight. Like a moth drawn to light, I stopped to admire it, and I suddenly remembered that Grandfather used to scold me for staring.

My mother's shadow moved across an inside wall of the tent in the candlelight, and she appeared beside my father. She put a hand on his shoulder, and lovingly thumbed its blade; then my father covered the hand that was stroking him with his own, and put it to his lips.

"I want to go back to India," my father murmured, his hand still covering that of my mother, his face turned upward to hers.

My mother started slightly backwards in her confusion and frowned, "What do you mean, back to India?"

There was a brief moment of silence between them. My father surreptitiously cleared his throat. "You know why, my darling."

I heard my mother draw a tiny, sharp breath, as she often did when annoyed.

"No," she said, as if that was the end of the conversation.

"Mary…" my father said kindly.

"No. Evelyn. No." My mother persisted.

There was a discomforting note of denial in my mother's voice, and it quivered as she spoke. Then, I heard her swallow as she lifted her hand to her throat, her eyes wide and bright with frustration.

My father heaved a heavy sigh. It was hard to argue with my mother and hope to win, but it must have been important to him to win this particular argument. He threw a look out the window and, even though I think he saw me anyway, I ducked and sat hugging my knees tightly, as if to hide myself, in plain sight.

"I just think it's the right thing to do," my father said.

"You've only been back there once, *thirty years ago*."

"But Mary, if I'm going to…"

A loud smacking sound rang through the tent as my mother slammed her hands down on my father's makeshift desk. "Don't," she growled.

"Ugh, Mary!" My father bellowed.

I stood up slowly and, with my hands on the tent window, I peeped inside.

"One day, Mary, you'll have to face the fact that I'm not going to live forever. I'll be lucky if I live beyond next Christmas, so the least you could do is, if you love me, *face reality* and let me die where I was born."

"You…" My mother's voice was losing the battle not to quiver. She cleared her throat, "You are not going to die. I won't let you. Think of our daughter. Think of Margaret."

I knew my mother was right. It was an instinct my father had, but who could say instinct was always right? I sat back in the dirt and closed my eyes as I tried to calm my racing, anxious mind.

"Mags?"

It was Mae. I was so busy eavesdropping that I mustn't have noticed her brief disappearance. She had never called me Mags before. It made me forget my parents, and I smiled. "U. Adebayo and Grace say I come fetch you."

U is the Burmese word for 'Mister.' I remembered Mr. Pang using it when addressing a man in Burma, pronouncing it 'Oo.'

"Where your Mama and Papa?"

Mae and I crept inside the tent. We found my father casually sprawled on his camp bed, the crook of his elbow resting on his forehead, one knee bent, his eyes closed. I wondered if he was in pain.

My mother appeared behind me and handed my father

a glass of water.

"Daddy?" I said timidly, "Is something wrong?"

"No, darling," breathed my mother with a smile anyone could see through.

"It's fine, Mags," said my father.

Mae marched up to my father and tugged at his arm. "Uncle Jones! Mr. Adebayo say Maggies to come quickly! He has big, good surprise!"

My father chuckled softly, looking his old self again, "Is that so?" he smiled wryly, "Well, you'd best head off, hadn't you?"

With my father's nod of approval, Mae and I raced out of the tent to find Grace.

Through the camp and down a steep, winding path lined with African oil palms, Grace led us to our surprise. The general scent of elephants was in the air, pungent as if they were standing right in front of us. We were met by Mr. Adebayo at the top of the path, who wore a knowing smile as he watched us coming toward him.

The elephants here sounded different to the ones in Burma. They were much bigger, and somehow that made them sound louder. Their beds were made of long flattened grass, and the first thing we saw when we drew close was a mother elephant surrounded by the rest of the herd; she was circling, like a dog chasing its tail in slow motion. There was something white and shiny coming from her behind. She was trumpeting loudly and painfully as she bent on her hind legs, then her front legs. Then she stood up again, and a torrent of water flowed from behind her.

"She's having baby!" Mae gasped, pointing.

"Should we get help?" I said excitedly.

"No," replied Mr. Adebayo, with a watchful eye on the elephants, "She can do it herself. She has her family with her."

The new mother elephant stomped her front feet on the spot and puffed air through her huge, magnificent trunk. Then a shiny mass dropped, quite unceremoniously, to the ground and a newborn baby hatched from its sack.

The four of us gasped loudly, almost in time with the herd as they trumpeted joyfully at the birth of their new family member. The newborn calf flailed about, seemingly unaware of its legs.

Then his mother nudged him upward. He stood wobbling as his trunk went in search of something to eat, grasping at his mother's leathery hide before finding the teat. We watched as he suckled greedily.

Grace, Mae and I skipped back toward camp, hand in hand and humming nothing particular. We felt overjoyed with happiness at being able to witness the incredible miracle of birth unfolding before our eyes.

As we approached the campsite, something suddenly

awful dawned on me. *Was my father dying? How did he know? How could he be sure?*

I needed to hear the reassuring hum of my father's voice. "Daddy…?"

He was working, and reams of paper seemed to be piling up beside him on his desk, with the odd black journal poking out, unsteadily balanced beneath the piles. I usually never liked to disturb him when he was writing, and I would likely be scolded for eavesdropping but I had to know why he wanted to go to India.

"Yes, my love?" He said, clearing his throat.

I dragged my eyes around the tent. It was furnished almost like a real house, with an ottoman in the corner here and a side table there. I noticed a replica of the globe from our library at home, and went over to it, spinning it carefully. It revolved slowly, and then my father's hand came down and stopped it.

"You want to know where India is, don't you?" he said knowingly, raising a wry eyebrow.

I nodded. My father crouched beside me and took the little globe with both hands. His eyes and hands rested there for a long while, and a smile flashed on his wide mouth, as if he were God marvelling at his own creation. He pointed to a spot and whispered, "Just here. Do you see?"

It wasn't as far from Africa to India as it was from

England to Burma. My father smiled, this time because my face was glowing with the excitement of a new adventure, as it always did.

"Daddy…?" I said, shyly, "Are you dying?"

He didn't answer straight away. His eyes sunk into my face. My eyes resembled his, housing a deep desire for life and hunger for knowledge, old and new. I had a feeling I knew the answer to my question, but I wanted to hear it, anyway.

He combed his fingers through my hair and swept my cheek, lovingly thumbing my chin. "No, my love," he said, almost in a whisper, "Not if I can help it, anyway."

"When do we go?" I asked, all of a sudden desperately worried and excited at once. "Is Mae coming with us? And Mr. Pang? What about George?"

My father chuckled softly, "Don't worry," he said, "they'll all be there."

He gathered me in his arms and held me close. He made to let me go, but then returned to holding me. With my head on his shoulder, I looked up and saw my mother standing in the doorway. She smiled at me and silently took her leave.

"We saw a baby elephant being born," I said excitedly.

My father gasped in excitement, "So, that was Mr. Adebayo's surprise, eh? How *wonderful*, my darling!"

"I'm going to come back as an elephant," I said, setting my chin proudly.

"What a marvellous idea," my father said with an affirmative bob of the head, "Perhaps I will, too."

CHAPTER 19

The next morning, I woke to the pitter-patter of rain outside. My parents had woken before me; my father was already writing, and my mother was curled up on the ottoman with a book, her feet tucked under her; she didn't seem genuinely invested in her book, however. Her eyes were resting on one page, but she didn't seem to be reading.

I swung out of bed and went to the window to look out at the weather, which must have decided to follow us from England. I huffed. *We didn't come here to be indoors!* I screamed internally, *we came here to see cheetahs and zebras!*

I twisted to look at the wireless on my father's folding desk. It was a convenient little appliance, well-suited to travel with us wherever we went. I tiptoed across the room and, slightly unfamiliar with the inner workings of this wireless radio, I glanced over it.

Ah. There it is. I twisted the large knob on one side, and the sweet, melodic voice of Vera Lynn filled the tent with the song, *We'll Meet Again.* I closed my eyes and, clutching my heart with both hands, I waltzed myself around the room.

Then I felt a pair of hands unfurl my own and hold them. I opened my eyes to find the blurry world spinning like a merry-go-round before me. My father met my disorientated face and placed a hand on my back, the other holding mine as he took the lead. He spun me into my mother's arms, and I danced from one to the other, all of us happy in our shelter from the rain.

When the rain had eased, I ventured out with an umbrella to visit the newborn baby elephant with Grace and Mae.

"They want to take me to India," I blurted out as we trekked through the muddy path to the elephants. I wanted to keep it to myself, but felt desperate to find comfort in my friends.

"*India*?" exclaimed Grace.

"Why?" asked Mae.

"I don't know." I shrugged.

"That seem long way away," said Mae.

"It isn't," I said.

"Oh," Grace replied, sounding forlorn.

I explained that my father was born there, that I had never been, that I had seen pictures of the Taj Mahal, and that I knew they worshipped cows.

"In Burma, we worship phoenix," said Mae.

"I don't know if we worship any animals," Grace added,

seeming curious and surprised.

"When?" asked Mae.

I shrugged once more in uncertainty. "I wish *you* could come with us," I told Grace.

Grace shrugged. "Maybe we'll meet again one day."

I smiled. I heard the words of a song floating in the air, and I hoped with all my heart that she was right. *'We'll meet again, don't know where, don't know when…'*

CHAPTER 20

In the days that followed, my friends and I spent every spare moment with the mother elephant and her newborn calf. We were supervised, of course, Mr. Adebayo wasn't taking any chances with these seemingly gentle animals. Even as children, we understood the unpredictability of wild animals by now.

My father and George had worked each day, taking turns to record the calf's measurements, height and weight, that is, how much it ate and how often, and made sure that Dorothy, as we had named the mother, was doing her job sufficiently.

Before I knew it, the day came for us to depart for India. I didn't know what to expect, but it was a new adventure, so I tried my best to embrace the mixture of excitement and trepidation I was feeling. *A quick goodbye is a good goodbye.* Or so I have heard. But is it?

We were travelling back to Cape Town to catch the ferry; from there, we would go to Bombay and then travel by rail to Kerala, where my father was born.

As I sat on my packed trunk in the empty tent, I felt hot in my travelling coat, and the pins in my hair under my blue felt hat made my head itch. *Why do I have to wear a coat to travel in?* I wondered irritably.

"Mags?" My father offered me a loving smile, "Come on. It's almost time."

I threw myself dramatically backwards on my trunk, lying like a dead body over the top. I opened one eye and saw my father marching toward me with a wry expression. "You can't take a dead body on a boat," I challenged, "they'll hang you, or something."

My father snorted with quiet amusement. "I see all this travelling's brought out the dark side of you, Mags. Whatever would your mother say?"

I shut my eyes tightly and folded my arms. Then my father's loud exclamation of "*AHEM!*" caused me to open my eyes. He stood over me with his hands on his hips, his head tilted and one eyebrow raised. His mouth curved into a cynical smile.

"What's the matter?" he sighed, grabbing the toe of my boot and wiggling it as he would one of my toes.

I huffed. "I don't want to leave."

He smiled at me. "You never want to leave."

That isn't true. I wanted to leave Barkings.

"Well," I offered, "this time I really, really, *really don't want to leave."* I said, straining my voice at the close of my argument for effect.

My father crouched beside me, and I finally pulled myself up to sitting, choosing to listen.

"Maggie," he said, placing a huge hand over my tiny kneecap, "You're going to love India. Especially where we're going, it's unbelievably beautiful."

"How do you know?" I said, not meaning it, "You haven't been back in 30 years."

"Hmm," said my father, recognising the deliberate sarcasm in my tone, but choosing to ignore it, "well, I might have known when you were born you were going to be your mother's parrot."

"Sorry," I whispered, almost inaudibly. I meant it this time.

My father took my hands and gave them an affectionate squeeze.

"Trust me, my darling, this is going to be an adventure *just* as wonderful as the others."

Mr. Adebayo stuck his head through the opening of our now empty tent and told us to meet him at base camp as he had one last surprise for us. So, when we had packed the Rover, we made our way to base camp.

As we drew close, we heard the sound of drums, wind

instruments, and women's voices harmonizing, as if getting ready to perform.

Then, we saw it. A whole community of local men and women in splendid traditional African dress of bright colours, all dancing, playing instruments and singing in our honour.

Mr. Adebayo was among them, dressed in a beautiful robe of orange and blue. He played an African drum, with three other men in similar dress. The women had ribbons with bells tied around their ankles; they all whooped and cheered as they sang and chanted.

Grace was dancing, too, and she broke from her bandmates to pull Mae and me into the celebration. "Come on!" she cried, her voice brimming with excitement. "It's easy! Follow me!"

She was right. It was easy to leap about joyfully and shriek with delight; even the African lyrics were easy to pick up, and even Mae was singing by the end. I danced with my friends in laughter, song, and unity.

I closed my eyes to harness the memory of the two best friends I had ever had, with the exception of my father.

No, my ever-present conscience sounded.

Don't think of Daddy. This. This right now is all that matters. For now, anyway.

And so, we said goodbye to our new African friends.

While it felt as though we had only been there a short time, my parents and I had made a home in Africa. I wondered if we carry the memory of a place with us, as you do after a person dies. Could you carry a place with you? I hoped so.

PART 3

INDIA

CHAPTER 21

The swell of the ocean was substantial when we arrived at the docks of Cape Town. The sky was a strange, dark bluish-grey, the waves were choppy and unforgiving, but there was no rain, just a threatening promise of a later deluge.

As we climbed the gangplank, the roped guardrail quivered in the breeze. My father went first, and my mother held my hand tightly; she wasn't a confident sailor at the best of times, but the huge swell and threat of a storm made her anxious.

We made our way to our cabin, which was comfortable and made warm by being shut up since the last passengers had docked.

My poor mother was instantly seasick and disappeared into the tiny adjoining bathroom. I claimed a bed and sat down, covering my ears with the pillow to drown out the sound of my mother's violent illness.

My father seemed to be worsening too, though not as much as my mother. He sank to the remaining bed, and with elbows on his knees, he dropped his head between his legs. I looked around, the last man standing, desperate to make the waves stop.

I fell to my knees by my bed and clasped my hands together. *"Hail Mary, full of Grace, the lord is with thee. Blessed art thou among women and blessed is the fruit of thy…"*

"Margaret," my father snapped in whisper.

"… the fruit of thy womb, Jesus." My conscience finished for me.

"What on earth are you doing?" my father questioned, baffled.

I shrugged. He sighed and stretched at full length on the bed before closing his eyes. Then my mother emerged, dabbing her mouth lightly with her handkerchief.

"We're in for a long week, Mags," my father said, drunk with nausea.

Within a few minutes, my parents were asleep. Just as well, I reflected. I wondered if Mae & Mr. Pang's cabin was the same as ours and if, like me, Mae wasn't feeling the effects of the swaying world outside the ferry.

The ferry rocked heavily as it bravely left the dock, pushing through the monstrous waves.

There were a lot of Indian people aboard, I assumed most likely returning home from holidays and business. Their language was quite pretty, I thought, listening now and then to the conversations they had with each other.

The ferry was full of colourful saris and sparkling jewels. The sweet sound of tiny bells from the gold chains around the women's ankles as they walked up and down the boat to stretch their legs reminded me of sleigh bells at Christmas.

Three days or so into our journey, as the sun was out and the upper deck dry, Mae and I were walking amongst the chiming ankle bracelets and colourful garments when we saw an old Indian lady on a deck chair. She was dressed in a beautiful red sari embroidered with fruiting vines of gold thread, and smoking a long pipe that billowed with smoke.

I had always been told it was rude to stare, and I agreed, but Mae and me couldn't help ourselves, the plume of smoke coming from the pipe was mesmerising to us and the smell it emitted was intoxicating.

"Excuse me?" I said, as politely as I knew how, "but, may I ask, what is that?"

"It is hashish, little girl," she replied to my surprise, in perfect English.

"What *hashish*?" demanded Mae, rude as ever.

"You should mind your own business," the lady snapped, inhaling deeply. "Now bugger off, the pair of you!"

Mae and I sniggered loudly and backed away as the Indian lady tilted her head back and blissfully closed her eyes, seeming unaffected by our abrupt interaction. When I finally stopped staring, I turned to find Mae rummaging through a hessian rucksack under the deck chair the lady occupied.

"*Mae!*" I hissed, "what are you doing?!"

Mae whisked a small leather pouch from the bag, her eyes bright with mischief.

"I want to try hashish!" she whispered. "Look at her! She looks happy!"

Mae broke open the pouch and carefully pinched the odd moss-like substance inside. She rummaged further and let out a small triumphant gasp, pulling free a small pipe along with a box of matches.

Before I could rebut, Mae grabbed my hand and plonked us down on a deck chair a few metres away. She struck a match with a quick flick. The sharp scent of the match stung my nose as she lit the bowl and drew in a shaky breath before passing it to me.

I hesitated, but her expectant grin left me little choice. I pressed my lips to the pipe and inhaled, the smoke bitter and heavy as it caught in my throat. We passed it between us in nervous giggles, unaware of exactly what we were doing, taken over by recklessness abandonment.

At first, I felt nothing, just a horrible taste on my tongue and a warmth that crept slowly through my body. But then the deck seemed to shift under me, and the colours of the world thickened, as if painted in strokes too vivid to belong to reality. Mae and I collapsed back into the deck chair, clutching our sides as laughter spilled out of us in sudden, senseless bursts, neither of us knowing why.

I remember some strange dreams I had while I lived at Barkings but they were nothing compared to the hallucinations I seemed to be experiencing now.

I was surrounded by floating saris, covering my vision like a patchwork quilt to the tune of maniacal laughter that what little part of my rational brain told me was the laughter of happiness. Still, my thumping chest alerted me to semi-consciousness where I could hear the muffled voices of my parents, Mae, George and Mr. Pang floating above me, trying to pull me out of whatever dark abyss this was.

Then the hallucinations materialised. Elephants swam in the air, some somersaulting, others calling out to me, like in my dreams at Barkings.

I heard Mr. Pang's voice shouting and scolding her in English, saying, "Look at her! How could you do this to your friend?!"

I felt the warmth of my father's calloused, shaking hand on my cheek. I stopped giggling as my parent's voices called me. I blinked myself back to reality and onto deck.

"Maggie?" My mother said, clearly distressed.

I turned to see her crouched beside me, opposite my

father. Mae, George and Mr. Pang were gathered around me too.

"I say, Lady Mags!" George exclaimed, "There's an experience you won't forget in a hurry."

My mother jabbed George in the side with her elbow. I felt the ferry spinning and swaying at the same time. I sat up in a panic, a little too fast for my insides, "Get a bucket or something, for God's sake!" barked my father.

George came to my rescue with a bucket, the contents of which he unceremoniously dumped overboard. I exploded with sickness. The torrent of spew seemed endless, robbing me of the entirety of my stomach contents, or so it seemed.

I slipped into something like semi-consciousness, and someone scooped me up into weightlessness and carried me away, but where they took me, I didn't know.

Hours later, I woke in our cabin, unaware of how long I had been asleep. I could hear the ship's engine gently whirring and churning the seawater below. I felt but too sick to think of putting anything in my mouth; even the thought of food made me gulp in an attempt not to vomit again.

I could hear my parents and the Indian lady's whispered voices coming from the corridor.

"We're terribly sorry, Mrs. Ganeesha," I heard my mother's voice say, "We'll do our best to explain to the children how wrong they were."

"I understand perfectly, Mrs. Jones," Mrs. Ganeesha replied, "I only hope your little girl is alright?"

I frowned. What about Mae? I sat up, and for some reason, I looked around as if I might find her there, but nothing.

When I felt strong enough, I crept across the room and opened the door to find my parents and Mrs. Ganeesha suddenly staring at me in surprise.

"Oh, Mags!" my mother exclaimed, folding me in her arms, "that was *such* a silly thing to do, why did you do it?"

"I...I don't know," I said. I really didn't know.

"Well, you and Mae are in a world of trouble, you know that, don't you?" my father said, stern but clearly concerned.

"Yes, Daddy," I said apologetically, "Is Mae alright? Can I go see her?"

My father nodded and pointed in the direction of Mae's cabin, ushering me to go and see her. As I tiptoed up the ship's corridor, the melodic sound of Mae singing 'Twinkle, Twinkle, Little Star' in Malay filled my relieved heart.

"Mae?" I said, carefully pushing her cabin door open.

I found her sprawled upside down on the bed, joyfully singing away.

"Hey...!" she said accusingly, as if I wasn't allowed to be there; then her legs shot into the air and she slid off the bed. Her head made an unholy crack as it met the floor.

"Ow!" she exclaimed and bobbed up to sitting.

"Are you alright?" I said as I sat down beside her.

"Yes," she shrugged, "maybe we not smoke hashish again."

We both laughed, but it was the nervous kind that faded quickly into silence. In the days that followed, we kept mostly to ourselves, each of us nursing a private shame. Meals were eaten under the watchful eyes of our parents, and whenever Mrs. Ganeesha passed, Mae and I lowered our gazes, guilt pressing almost heavier than our embarrassment.

By the time the ship slowed into the harbour, our mischief felt like a distant shadow.

We arrived in Bombay on a Monday afternoon. The air was filled with a pinkish-orange haze, and the heat waved at us in the distance, making the palm trees dance behind it. It wasn't long before a large black cab came toward us.

The cab driver loaded our trunks into the boot and we began our short journey to the train station. The road was dusty, alive with traffic and cattle, people walking by, beggars selling all manner of things to everyone who passed them. People honked their horns loudly, but, as our driver explained, was more a sign of goodwill, rather than road rage.

Suddenly, he slowed and wound down his window, passing a handful of shiny silver shillings to a beggar in exchange for a generous bunch of bananas.

"Better wind up your window, Sahib," he turned and said to my father, "if you give money to one, they all come."

How curious to say such a thing, I thought, then before I knew it, several beggars appeared in front of our cab, crowding it with their begging and offerings. Faces pressed against our windows, hands reaching for us, voices rose and fell in a language that seemed both harsh and musical. The air was heavy with spice and smoke, alive with colour and noise, and I felt as though we had stumbled into another world entirely.

I buried my face in my father's shirt and felt his hand on my head; my mother was clinging tightly to his arm on the other side. Our driver shouted at the beggars in Punjabi, and as if by magic, they slowly dispersed. We all breathed a sigh of relief, and our cab crawled slowly up the road through the thickest traffic I had ever seen.

This was our introduction to India; chaotic, bewildering, and unforgettable. A culture shock that left me both frightened and strangely fascinated all at once.

CHAPTER 22

The train station hummed like an enormous beehive of angry bees. Rail workers barked at porters like angry dogs, and the porters ran around like blue-arsed flies, as my grandfather would have called them.

We weaved our way through the manic swarms, all crammed like tinned sardines in what I thought was a large railway station, but the people made it seem smaller than the rabbit hole.

My parents led the way, each holding my hand as we walked single file toward the train. Mae was riding on Mr. Pang's shoulders, and George was behind us, carrying my mother's, mine, and his own trunks. Lucky for him, they were small trunks. Still, we could only see his legs working furiously under the load in his arms.

It was noisy. The voices of a million people echoed through a small space, which seemed to die down at the shriek of a whistle, heralding the slow arrival of what looked like a train miles long. It reminded me of the Orient Express. I could see passengers standing up in their cabins, all impatient to disembark. A rail worker marched the length of the tracks, blowing his whistle and waving everyone off the train, directing them safely away.

"Move!" Someone with a thick Punjabi accent shouted in the crowd. "Step away from the track, do you want to get crushed to death?!"

I grimaced. Then the crowd began to move forward to climb into the train. My father scooped me up and led my mother by the hand inside the locomotive.

Inside, it was peaceful, but still crowded. Much worse than outside, but at least no one was shouting as much. A pleasant hum of chatter filled the long corridor, and I was surprised to see so many white people amongst the natives. There seemed to be harmony between whites and Hindus. Then I remembered, *of course. Queen Victoria was the Empress of India.*

"Well!" George huffed with relief, "Kerala, here we come, eh?"

My father ushered my mother to an empty booth. My mother sat down heavily and mopped her brow with her handkerchief. George and Mr. Pang sat opposite us, took out a chess set, and started a game. My father took out a volume of Rudyard Kipling, which I thought quite appropriate, and Mae and I jumped into a seat and turned to the window to look out.

It was almost like the traffic on the road. People swarmed the railway, selling things to the rich, begging, and busking. There was a snake charmer who quickly disappeared behind a small, rushing crowd. Someone jumped off the tracks onto the platform as the train began to move, then another, like flowers sprouting from the dirt. There was a faint whiff of coal from the train's engine, mingled with dust spices, fish and meat from vendors selling their wares wherever they could.

The sound of chanting carried from a temple in the distance to our train as we left the city, passing cows grazing on hay and other dried grass which sprouted from the hard earth. People waved as we went past, mostly because we waved at them. We stuck our heads out the window and looked up to see a large group of people, including women and children, sitting on the train's roof.

"They will fall off!" Mae exclaimed.

"No, they won't," I said, "I bet they do that all the time!"

A breeze picked up as we gained speed, and while the air wasn't as fresh as the jungles of Burma or Africa, it was thick with dust and steam from the train. I shut my eyes and quickly closed the window.

The nighttime hours brought peace to the train carriages, but they remained busy. The train walls were not thick enough to block out the noise of the cabin next door. *At least my parents don't snore*, I thought, listening to the person in the next cabin snoring louder than I had ever heard before.

In the morning, we stopped to collect passengers. As the new passengers piled on board, my father took Mae and me to see if we could find a way onto the top of the train.

Of course, there was one, in the shape of a little ladder screwed onto the outer walls of the train.

"We can ride up here if you like," My father said, always enthusiastic about making anything an adventure.

"Oh, Daddy, can we?!" I replied excitedly.

"Yes, Uncle, please, we can ride on the roof?!" Mae chimed in.

My father and I both fixed Mae with a look of astonishment. *"What?"* said Mae, shrugging one careless shoulder, "You Uncle, isn't you?"

It was hard to be unforgiving of Mae's sweet, broken interpretation of the King's English and her careless attitude toward anything anyone said or did. My father broke into an enormous smile, took Mae's face in both hands, and kissed her forehead.

"Bless you, Mae Wen Pang," he whispered, *"my darling girl. Don't ever change."*

"EUGHH!" Mae exclaimed, swiping her forehead.

"Come on!" I said, seizing Mae's hand.

I climbed the ladder's first rung, and the white linen of my father's shirt brushed against my rear. The train was moving fast, and for some reason, while I had initially been excited about the idea of riding on the roof of a moving train, now that I was on the ladder, my nerve seemed to abandon me; "Daddy…!" I whispered unconsciously, hoping that he would be ready to catch me if I fell, which he was.

"It's alright," he whispered back, and I felt his cheek brush against my back as he checked that everything was sound.

My palms started to sweat. Even though it wasn't that far up, it certainly felt it. My father slid an arm around my middle from behind.

"Mags?" came a disturbed voice from below, "Evelyn, where are you?"

My mother let out a sharp gasp, which made me almost lose my footing. I couldn't see her, but I could feel her concern.

My father looked down as we almost reached the top.

"What on earth are you three doing?" My mother shouted.

"Climbing!" My father responded happily, "Come on up, my love!"

"Have you *lost your mind*?!"

"Yes!" said my father, teasing, his voice straining under my weight as he lifted me, "damned inconvenient, I think I must have dropped it somewhere between Botswana and Bombay!" he added playfully.

"No more sense than you were born with!"

I smiled to hear my mother's gentle voice, which, try as she might, she could not hide, even when trying to keep us all safe and in line.

Mae and I giggled with amusement. I felt my father's hand cup my bottom and hoist me up over the last rung of the ladder. Mae appeared beside me, and we staggered as we found our footing.

People spread for miles, seated with crossed legs on the roof. My father came up behind us and hooked his arms around our waists to sit us down. I sat hugging my knees, the wind in my hair, my eyes closed, a wide smile across my face.

"Look at that, my love," my father said to my mother, "have you ever seen anything like it?"

"No..." My mother replied, unable to hide the amazement, "I haven't."

I heard the sound of kissing and turned to see my father wrapping my mother in his arms from behind. The pins in my mother's hair had come loose, stray hairs brushed his cheek as she rested her head on his chest. He brushed her hair smooth and tenderly kissed her shoulder.

Mae put an arm around me and touched her head to mine. Then I realised, Mae was fast asleep.

CHAPTER 23

We arrived in Kerala at dawn. When I woke, my parents were already fussing about, tidying themselves up, preparing to disembark. My mother hurried me out of bed and immediately began brushing my hair a little too violently.

"Ouch!" I hissed.

My mother grabbed my chin and pulled my face up to hers; "Ouch!" I said again.

"Right," Mummy huffed, "let me look at you. Good." And she patted my cheek and brushed my shoulders and arms of whatever dust she imagined might be there.

When we were respectable, we filed out of the cabin into the corridor where a line of passengers had already formed. Some were very pushy and bumped into us with their hard leather cases.

My parents pulled me closer to them, for my safety. I turned to try to see where Mae and the others were but the thousands upon thousands of bodies blocked my view. Still, I could hear Mae shouting with all the strength of her God-given lungs, not caring to whom she spoke, clearly shouting at everyone to get out of her way.

It made me smile. My little friend was not as forcefully polite as any British person; she knew how to handle herself in a crowd.

"I say?!" called George. We all turned to see where his voice had come from. A hand with a wristwatch and its band of faded brown leather shot up, clutching a rail ticket. "I say, Evelyn?!" He trotted toward us now, weaving his way through the boundless sea of bodies as politely as he could.

"I say!" George exclaimed when he had almost caught his breath, "Not exactly Paddington Station, is it?"

We all chuckled, and when Mae and Mr. Pang caught up to us, we seemed to be stuck in the middle of a slowly dispersing crowd. The smell of perspiring bodies was overwhelming but was replaced by fresh air as the crowd dispersed.

The gentle putt-putting of a car engine brought our attention to the road behind us, and a gigantic blue motorcar pulled onto the curb; My father's ayah's husband came to take us to his house from the station. My grandfather had left his home to my father's ayah in his will, and so, when Uncle Singh, as my father called him, got out of his big old car to meet us, it was like meeting family.

"My dear Evan!" exclaimed Uncle Singh, in a voice I could only describe as smooth hot cocoa, deep, inviting, and comforting. He approached my father with open arms and swept his cheeks with big, strong hands.

"Uncle Singh," said my father, smiling brightly, "this is Margaret, my daughter."

He turned toward me with a rather grand gesture, as though announcing royalty.

"Ah," said Uncle Singh, a broad smile of brilliant white teeth spreading across his face. "*Princess* Margaret. How wonderful to meet you."

We loaded our cases into the back of the car, and once we were all settled, we pulled away from the station, the din of the crowd fading behind us. The journey took us out of the bustle and into the countryside, where the landscape shifted to wide, open spaces and a blur of green.

The scent of earth and tea leaves filled the air. At last, we arrived.

Uncle Singh had turned my grandfather's house into a tea plantation with my grandfather's blessing. The house stood near the water, surrounded by tall palm and avocado trees. The tea plants spread for miles, climbing up the slopes in neat rows like green stairways. Neighbouring cattle who grazed in Uncle Singh's fields, seemed unbothered by our arrival.

At the front door, Uncle Singh's wife, Raksha, stood waiting for us. He had insisted I call her *Aunty* Raksha. She was dressed to meet us in a beautiful red sari, golden bracelets and armbands, gold slippers and a little decorative mark of white paint on her forehead. She stepped forward and embraced us each in turn, her warmth immediate and sincere.

"This is as much our home as it is ours," she said, her voice as soft as her husband's was rich. "If not more."

We were shown to our rooms and given time to unpack our bags and take a moment after our long journey.

Before long, the faint scent of spices drifted through the house from the kitchen, encouraging my stomach to moan with hunger. In the evening, we enjoyed a supper of spiced roasted vegetables, dahl, yoghurt and rice, with black tea and a drink made of yoghurt called lassi. Mae and I sat wide-eyed, listening as my father and Uncle Singh traded stories - tales of my grandfather and his adventures around the globe.

After supper, my father and Uncle Singh stayed up and drank port, while Aunty Raksha whisked Mae and I away to bathe. The tub was made of gold-plated tin, and I stood watching as the hot water filled it to half-mast.

I turned to Mae, who was bashfully concealing her tiny breasts with her arms crossed. I thought of the time she had stripped by the waterhole in Burma, and chortled to believe that she was shy now.

"Okay, Missy Sahib!" said Aunty Raksha, pumping her

fingers at us, "let's step out of those clothes and I will wash them!"

Mae stepped tentatively into the bath as I stepped out of my dress and underwear. I stepped into the tub, where Mae was already luxuriating. The water was hot, and the steam clung instantly to my face, coating me in beads of sweat. Mae pegged her nose and inhaled deeply, disappearing into the carbolic, white water.

Aunty Raksha grabbed my head and yanked it slightly to one side, and began scrubbing hard with the soap. I winced as strands of hair snapped under the thick bar of soap; then she took her hands and rubbed hard. When she had finished, she took a hard-bristled scrubbing brush and scrubbed my skin raw; I turned and saw Mae's horrified face. She was next.

After our not-so-relaxing wash, we stood, naked and barefoot, on the tiled floor. Aunty Raksha draped thin towels over us and rubbed our shoulders. "Okay!" she barked, "Bed!"

After we dressed and relaxed into bed as instructed, Mae fell asleep almost instantly. I, as usual, was too excited to close my eyes, but it was peaceful here; so quiet, I thought. I had gotten used to the sounds of the jungle and far-off voices, still busily going about their business. Here, the sound of chirping frogs, crickets, and the gentle, warm breeze whispering through the light curtains, was deafening.

Mae began to snore in a gentle, but still unladylike fashion. *Good,* I thought, *noise at last.*

Just then came a *knock*, the gentle rapping of knuckles on the door. "Come in?" I whispered.

It was my father. He smelt of whiskey and Old Spice mixed with perspiration. He had his hand behind his back and a suspicious smile on his face. I sat up in bed, and pulled the coverlet over myself for comfort.

"I've got something for you," he said, followed by a seemingly long silence, "close your eyes."

I shut my eyes and held out my hand for the surprise. Something small but heavy dropped into my cupped palms. I opened my eyes to see a red velvet ring box in my hands.

"What is it?" I asked, excitedly.

"It wouldn't be a surprise if I told you, would it?" he replied mischievously.

I cracked open the little box. Inside was a gold ring, set with a giant emerald.

"What's *this*?" I gasped.

"That, my darling, belonged to my mum, your Granny," my father explained, "it was her engagement ring. I want you to have it."

"But…" I ventured, confused, "but it won't fit me."

My father gave a soft chuckle. He stared at me momentarily and brushed my cheek, running his fingers through my hair.

"It'll fit you when you're older," he took my hand and

studied it for a long while, "you've got your grandmother's hands, you know?"

"How do you know?"

"You're very much like your grandmother," he said, matter-of-factly, "well, you make it easy to imagine what she was like when she was young, anyway."

A flicker of a smile lit his face, and he made to get up. "Sleep well, my love."

I opened my mouth to ask him why he had given me such a gift, but he was out the door before I got the chance.

CHAPTER 24

Morning came, and everyone agreed to have breakfast on the terrace that looked out onto the tea plantation. We dined on fruit, eggs, and potato cakes laced with spices and full of herbs and vegetables.

Uncle Singh told us his son, Taj, would be home from university soon. He attended Agra University and was studying horticulture. I of course, didn't know what a horticulturist was, but it sounded fascinating. I began to form a picture of Taj; if he was anything like Uncle Singh, he was handsome, I concluded.

After breakfast, Uncle Singh took us on a tour of the tea plantation. His car was like a Range Rover with an open top. Mae and I clung to the roof as we bumped along, standing on the back, sweeping through well-kept fields of fragrant tea trees. From the passenger seat, my father twisted to look at us, his arm resting casually on the back of his seat.

"See, Mags?" he said, "it's because of the Chinese and the Indians that we British have tea. What do you think of that?"

I giggled in the affirmative and turned to Mae; then, as all children surely do, we both burst into giggles for no reason but excitement. I turned to look at George, snapping picture after picture of the magnificent view.

Uncle Singh gestured passionately as he explained the tea-making processes in great detail, letting the leaves wither, rolling, tossing, and drying. All I wanted to know was when we would see a tiger.

"Where the tigers live?" Mae exclaimed as if she had read my mind.

Uncle Singh chuckled. "They are a safe distance away in the jungle, Miss Mae," he said kindly, "perhaps you will see them another time."

On our return to the house, we were in high spirits. Aunty Singh had set up tea on the terrace, and the sun was glowing a pinky-orange and yellow in the west, and it shone on the body of water the terrace overlooked.

As I climbed the three steps to the terrace, I saw the back of a tall, young man who must have had a cup of tea in his hand, for he slurped and said, "Ahh," as so many people do when they sipped tea they had been craving.

"Ah!" said Uncle Singh in surprise as his eyes lit up.

"Everyone, this is my son, Taj."

Taj turned over his shoulder to greet us, and my mouth

fell to my boots, not that he noticed straight away, thank heavens.

"Hello," he said, beaming a huge, white-toothed smile, like his father's.

"Margaret," whispered my father to get my attention. He winked when I looked at him, and demonstrated closing his mouth with a theatrical pop.

"Now!" said Uncle Singh, clapping Taj on the cheek, "I think Mami has made supper. Come!"

I could have listened to Taj talk about university, horticulture and the tea-making business for the rest of my life. He was intelligent, tall and muscular, with a whisp of dark stubble on his beautiful, coloured skin, a mass of wavy black hair, and eyes like bottomless black pools. I had always known about love from watching my parents, but the way Taj Singh made me feel was otherworldly.

I woke the next morning with the sound of a rooster and distant, lowing cattle. I blinked, and my ears perked at the sound of my father's typing. I smiled. It was a sound I hadn't heard in a long time.

Uncle Singh's hallway was bathed in bright white golden light, reflecting the morning sun on the white sandstone walls. I couldn't help but touch the framed paintings of the tea trees, the God Krishna, and scenes from the Ramayana, the story of

Rama and Sita. The sound of chanting and morning prayers hung in the air, and I crossed to the window to peer through the lattice carved appropriately into the shape of tea leaves and mango.

Taj was bathing in the stream. His naked back, rippled with pure muscle, was covered in droplets of water. It shone and glistened in the morning light.

"Taj?!" I called out, not knowing why and instantly regretting it.

Taj threw a careless look over his shoulder. I got the strangest inkling he hadn't seen me straight away, for he looked again, gasped in horror and dived into the water; then he sprang up like a breaching whale, let out a noise and shook like a wet dog, and I crept down the hill.

"Sorry," I said, trying to suppress a giggle, "did I frighten you?"

"No! *Yes*, I mean… what are you *doing here*?" he replied.

My mouth fell open. *What am I doing here*? I wondered. I looked around as if the answer might float conveniently past me so I could pluck it from the air, but no such luck.

"I-I- just wanted to come for a swim," was all I could come up with.

Taj caught his breath and swiped water from his face, his huge brown eyes stared and blinked at me, then raked me a little doubtfully.

"You are British," he pointed out unhelpfully, "can you even swim at all?"

"I *beg your pardon*?" I blurted out in a voice that sounded remarkably like my mother, "I'm ten years old, of course I can *swim*."

"Hah," said Taj in a tone of surprise, "Well, in that case, I apologise. I was under the impression that the British weren't very good swimmers."

"Well, that shows you haven't met many of us, doesn't it?" I said smartly.

A hint of a smile spread on Taj Singh's face. "Touche, Princess Margaret."

I smiled and made to turn back, then I looked over my shoulder. Taj was still looking at me, and for a fleeting moment, neither of us moved; Taj smiled at me, and I smiled back as I walked back up the hill toward the house.

Through the hallway, among the beautiful artworks, a tune entered my mind. A nameless, romantic piece of music I wasn't sure existed or if I had just made it up, but it made me smile. I waltzed up the hallway, imagining I was dancing with Taj.

CHAPTER 25

The following Tuesday, Uncle Singh took my father and Mr. Pang on a drive to the mangrove swamps where a family of tigers lived. It was the middle of the monsoon season, and the rain had been heavy for seven days.

I was never any good at Maths. My mind could never comprehend the power of symbols, the power they had to add, subtract and divide numbers to and from each other. The ferocity of the rain pelting down on the tiled roof was very distracting to my boundless imagination. I thought about the pictures of the tigers and monkeys in the hallway. Rama and Sita are all captured so beautifully that they could just about leap off the canvas and touch you, and in the case of the monkeys, jump all over you and mess up your hair as they groom you.

"Mags?" my mother's voice entered my consciousness.

I looked up at my mother, who was suddenly standing in front of me, bent slightly with her knuckles on the desk. "Jane has fifty apples and has to divide them between ten of her friends. How many does she have left?"

"What?" I said, not meaning to be rude.

My mother raised an eyebrow and tilted her head, as she often did when demonstrating her displeasure.

"Sorry," I murmured apologetically, "it's, uh, it's 5."

"Hmm," my mother replied, accepting my apology.

Mae gave me an ungentle jab in the ribs.

"What wrong?" she demanded, "You act strange at best of times, but this *crazy*!" she hissed, then leaning toward me, she said, "You tell me, I help you cheat."

"*Shh*!" I whispered, "I'll tell you later."

"Girls?" my mother snapped, "at least *try and concentrate*? Hmm?"

We turned to our work, but I was more reluctant than Mae. What was the point of Math anyway? What use were a bunch of numbers if I was going to be a nature conservationist? *Numbers are in everything*, Mags, said my father's voice, *just do your best.*

The ornate cuckoo clock in the corner of the living room ticked away. I dragged my gaze toward it and looked up. On the clock's head, was a monkey carved out of oak, its tail dangling toward the clock face. The clock's pendulum was a cheeky monkey swinging from a vine. I smiled, losing myself in the cheerful whimsy of the unusual timepiece.

Suddenly, we heard Uncle Singh's vehicle bumping up

the driveway. My father, Uncle Singh, and Mr. Pang were all drenched, smiling, joking and generally pleased with themselves after a good day's work.

"Hullo, my loves!" my father breathed as he marched in with open arms, taking my mother at arm's length and planting a rain-soaked peck on her cheek. He kissed me, his hands gripping my chin with enthusiastic affection.

"You're *soaked*!" my mother whined playfully.

"Ah! We work in all weathers, my love!"

He took my mother in his arms and swirled and dipped her like I imagined Fred Astaire had dipped Ginger Rogers while they danced the foxtrot. My parents looked much more beautiful together than Fred and Ginger, I thought so, anyway.

"Right..." my mother sighed as a smile flashed across her face, "girls, let's get back to our work."

CHAPTER 26

Mae and I were careless about the monsoon and its hidden dangers. We often took advantage of the flowing streams and waterholes around the plantation, for a little relief from the humidity the monsoon brought with it.

One day, while Mae and I sat paddling our feet at the water's edge, we looked up to see Taj coming down the hill, a long coil of rope slung over his shoulder. A tall oak stood nearby, its thick limb stretching conveniently over the deepest part of river.

"I've always wanted a rope swing!" Taj said, flashing a beautiful grin.

We watched as he got down on his knees and made a lasso, which, after measuring the distance from ground to limb, he swung a few times, then whoosh, tossed the rope upward and looped it around protruding limb. We all cheered as if it were the best thing we had ever seen.

"Watch this!" Taj shouted, clambering up the bank with the tail of the rope in his hand. He took a running start, then launched himself off the edge. "Whoo-hoo!" he yelled, swinging out wide before letting go and dive-bombing into the river with a great seismic splash.

Mae and I squealed with delight, cheering his efforts.

"Me next! Me next!" Mae cried, and before Taj could rebut, she grabbed the rope from him, climbed the bank, and pushed off, squealing joyously as she threw herself in.

"Come on, Maggies!" Mae exclaimed.

"Yes, come on, Princess Margaret!" Taj shouted, his lovely Hindi accent echoing in the peace of the plantation, "the water is dirty, but it is cleaner than you!"

He flashed a provocative smile, pegged his nose, and disappeared beneath the murky depths. I carefully climbed the bank, following the path made by Taj and Mae, gripping the rope with all my life. Once at the top, I dragged my gaze down the bank to the water, the tremble in my knees surely giving away my uncontrollable trepidation.

My concentration was broken by the sound of leaves crunching underfoot as Mae suddenly appeared beside me.

"I..." I whispered, winded, "I can't move."

"Why?" said Mae, shrugging carelessly, "You scared of height?"

"I-I don't know!"

"Looks to me like you scared height! Come on!" she encouraged.

"Mae...?" But before I knew it, Mae shoved me off

the edge. I swung in the air, legs flailing. I screamed. Then somehow my scream turned to squealing laughter.

"Let go, Princess Margaret!" Taj shouted.

I didn't want to let go. I closed my eyes and everything went green. Suddenly, I was in the tall trees, swinging from vine to vine with a troop of monkeys in the jungle, and when I opened them, the world streaked by. I was the pendulum of a grandfather clock, swaying back and forth. Then…

"Whoo-hoo!"

I let go. For a moment, my body fumbling through the air, weightless, wild. Then - *splash*! I hit the water in an explosion of sound and bubbles. From beneath the surface, I could just make out Mae and Taj cheering, their voices distant and distorted. I surfaced, gasping and laughing, then flopped onto my back like a whale's fin. As I floated, grinning from ear to ear, their whoops and cheers echoed across the plantation, muffled the water around me.

A massive wave of white rushed toward me. I made a face and shut my eyes tightly against Mae's splashing. I splashed her back and we giggled. Then another wave came toward me, and something lifted me out of the water and chucked me like a harpoon back in the water. I spun around and retaliated, splashing Taj with all the strength I had.

Later, we marched up the hill back toward the house, dripping, breathless, and full of joy. When we arrived, George and Mr. Pang were sitting on the terrace, locked in a game of chess. George, leaning forward on his elbow a bit like The Thinker, occasionally glanced sideways at Mr. Pang, it must have been his move.

"*Come on, Pang!*" George whispered impatiently.

"Maybe you shut up for two minutes, I can make my move?!" Mr. Pang exclaimed.

A playful smile spread on George's face. I heard the clicking of my father's typewriter. I left Mae and Taj and tiptoed up the hallway towards that tap, tap, tapping of the typewriter keys. I craned my neck to find my father at his desk. It's hard to describe the joy I got from seeing him at work; he wrote with such passion, and he was so quick with his fingers that it was almost like he was born with a typewriter for a twin.

He drew a sharp breath and fumbled in his sleeve for a handkerchief, coughed, sniffed heavily and tap, tap, tap, carried on working.

"Did you have fun down the river, Mags?" he inquired, not at me, but at the paper in his typewriter as he worked.

"Yes, Daddy."

"Good." *Tap, tap, tap, tap.*

I started with excitement. "Taj taught us how to swing from a rope into the river!" I exclaimed.

He gasped and raised his eyebrows theatrically. "Did

he? Did you have a go?"

"Mm-hm." I said, proudly.

He looked over the rim of his glasses at me. They were large, square tortoiseshell frames that made his almond-shaped brown eyes pop.

"And were you fearless?" he added, opening his arms.

I sat on his lap, and he wrapped his arms around me. "Mm-hm," I repeated.

"I'm glad," he said, "bravery's an important thing for people like you and me, isn't it?"

I nodded. "What are you writing about?" I said. I didn't know why, but until then, I had never been curious enough to ask. I just assumed I knew what he was doing because it was part of his job.

"I'm writing about our adventures," he explained casually, "so far."

I dragged my eyes down to the typewriter and touched the paper of coarse manila. The black letters faded in some places, lending the page a sweet personality; I didn't read the words, I was too inexplicably fascinated by the letters. The typewriter keys faded like the ones on the page from what some would call overuse, but my father called it passion.

"Do you think I could be a writer?" I said, fingering the keys like big buttons on a raincoat.

My father took off his glasses and flashed a smile. "You

can be whatever you want to be, my love, as long as you believe."

I looked over my shoulder and smiled brightly at him. He smiled back and lightly swept a hand from my shoulder to my elbow. He squeezed me affectionately, "come on, now," he said, playfully exaggerating his tough exterior, "let me get on with it. Go and play."

CHAPTER 27

The next morning, I woke as usual to the sounds of breakfast: hot water boiling for tea and bread frying in a pan with eggs and sausages. I also expected the clicking of typewriter keys, not today.

I tiptoed up the hallway, the floor creaking beneath my feet, when I heard my father's barking cough from my parents' bedroom. I looked in to see my father sitting on the bed with his back to me, my mother standing before him.

My mother took my father's face gently with both hands, drew him up to face her, and, eyeing him with critical concern, she swept his forehead. "It's nothing, my love," my father reassured her with breathless calm, "just a chest cold."

At tea time, Taj took it upon himself to arrange a game of cricket. We weren't much of a team in terms of size, but we made do. Taj was our batsman; George would bowl, and Mr. Pang playing as well, with Mae and me as umpires and second batsman.

My father watched from the terrace, reclining in a

large cane chair, playing with the white linen handkerchief my mother had made him when she was expecting me. My mother joined him on the terrace with a pitcher of lemonade, the golden juice glowing as the sun hit the glass jug.

Thwack went the ball as George bowled and Taj swung his bat.

"Oh! Shot!" George cried enthusiastically.

Two pairs of hands clapped along with the rest of us.

"Mags, *run*!" My father shouted. His voice was croaky, and he coughed a little. Suddenly excited, I broke and ran; I didn't know where, but running was fun. Everyone was shouting, "This way, Mags! No, that way!" and "Go, Mags! Run!" all at once.

With everyone pointing and shouting, clapping and cheering, I was giddy with joy, running between wickets. I touched the ground at either end of the pitch until I was told to stop, and collapsed in fits of giggles.

"Well done, Mags," my father called out.

"*Very* well done," added my mother.

I turned to my parents with a huge grin and a sense of achievement burning my cheeks. A similar sense of pride lit up my parents' faces as they clapped for me, giving me a standing ovation. But the joy was short-lived as I noticed my father struggling to breathe. His coughing and gasping became uncontrollable. Everyone dropped their bats and ran toward him as he sank to his chair, my mother holding his arm as the spasms racked his body.

"Get him inside," George ordered.

Aunty Raksha and Uncle Singh hurried out and helped my father inside. Mae, George and Mr. Pang gathered around to comfort me, the euphoria of my first cricket match melting like butter into bone-crushing fear.

"You not worry, Maggies," said Mae firmly, "Uncle Jones will be okay. Okay?"

She threw her arms around me, and I felt a hand wrap around my head and pull me close. I looked up and it was George. He was whispering soothing words that I couldn't hear above my thumping heart and the sobbing that had taken me without my knowing. I closed my eyes as tears rolled down my cheeks and onto my hands that I held together in prayer.

Please let it be alright.

Please let everything be alright…

CHAPTER 28

My father's coughing eventually settled, but now and then it would erupt again. The next day, the doctor came. I watched from my bedroom window as a large, blue motorcar swept elegantly up the driveway, its tyres like gentle rain on the loose gravel.

'*You must stay in your room when the doctor arrives,*' my mother had said, plainly not wanting me to catch anything or be seen in front of the important Dr. Varma.

But I couldn't help myself. When I knew my mother wasn't in the room, I tiptoed from the window to my bedroom door and quietly turned the knob. *Click* went the latch so that no one would know I had escaped.

I crept down the hallway and heard my father coughing again. I pushed at the bedroom door and peeped in.

"Oh… Mags," said my father, weakly, "come on in, my love." He was propped up by pillows in bed, clutching his hanky to his breast.

"Are you alright?" I asked timidly.

He smiled kindly at me. "Ah, I'm not too clever," he said honestly, "not to worry, my love. I'll be alright."

His hand lay open beside him, so I slid my hand, tiny in comparison, into his, and his fingers clenched over mine. A smile lit up his face momentarily. Then someone pushed the door open carefully. It was my mother.

"Evelyn? Dr. Varma is here."

I stood up and shyly bowed as Dr. Varma entered the room. My mother took a step aside, like someone opening the door for the king. My father pushed himself up on the bed and straightened the sheets to 'neaten' his appearance.

"Please," said the Indian doctor's voice, "Mr. Jones, don't sit upon ceremony. You must rest."

The rain had eased, and while the sound of it on the roof above us was pleasant, it paled compared to the sound of birds singing.

Dr. Varma's stethoscope shone in the sunlight. Dr. Varma was halfway through my father's examination when I wondered, *How does a stethoscope actually work?*

"Breath *in*..." Dr. Varma instructed softly.

My father inhaled deeply, and I heard the prickling in his lungs.

"Hmm," said Dr. Varma.

"What is it?" my mother asked anxiously.

"Mrs. Jones, I believe your husband has a collapsed

lung." The kind doctor responded.

"How?" my mother gasped.

"It can happen sometimes with coughing spasms," Dr. Varma explained, "you have had surgery recently to remove a tumour from your lungs, Mr. Jones?"

"Yes," croaked my father.

Dr. Varma nodded in understanding.

"What's to be done?" my mother asked, "How do we fix it?"

Dr. Varma reassured us that my father would get well and prescribed rest and little, preferably no, physical activity. I knew this would be torture for him. Childishly, he and I shared eye rolls, sighs and smiles when my mother and Dr. Varma weren't paying attention.

As midnight settled over the house, I drifted into a heavy sleep, Mae's unusually loud snoring filling the quiet. Hours later, I startled awake to the rasp of my father's coughing. Blinking against the dark, I sat up as the light in my parents' room spilled into the hallway.

Another violent spasm wracked him, the sound tearing through the stillness of the night. Heart racing, I scrambled out of bed, hurried across the room, and slipped into the hallway.

As I neared their doorway, my frantic run slowed to cautious, tiptoed steps. Inside, my mother was bent tenderly over my father, her hand softly stroking his forehead, her voice low and steady. My father lay on his side, coughing so violently it seemed as though each breath might be his last.

"Mummy?" I called.

"Go back to bed, Mags," she said, her voice tight with strain.

But I could see the towel clutched in her hands, stark white and blotched with what looked like blood. I backed away slowly and broke out suddenly in a cold, anxious sweat. Sliding beneath my covers once again, I lay shaking and scared for my family. *Would my father be alright? Would he ever get better?*

Sleep returned eventually, broken by the echo of coughs and my mother's whispering voice. By the time the first light of morning crept through my window, I felt worry and exhaustion overtake my mind.

At breakfast, we gathered on the terrace as usual. Mae, George, Mr. Pang and I tried to keep our chatter subdued, so as not to wake my parents. The mood was sombre as the uncertainty of my father's health pressed heavily on us all.

When my father eventually woke, just after mid-morning, he was horribly pale, with dark circles under his eyes, and his face shone with fever. He sat heavily beside me at the kitchen table where I was doing my school work, and leaned back in his chair, covering my hand with his and giving me his ever-loving smile.

"You look bloody awful," remarked George in a way he knew would make my father smile.

He let out a cautious chuckle that quickly dissolved into a harsh, painful cough. Grimacing, he rose abruptly and hurried inside. Moments later, the sounds of violent sickness reached us from within. When he finally emerged, he was wiping his mouth, his face pale and drawn.

The doctor came again after lunch. Mae and I waited outside with Taj. It was nice to have Taj there to support us, like a big brother, but all I could think about was my father, and I felt uneasy every time he coughed.

"Don't worry, Princess Margaret," said Taj, putting his arm around me and drawing me close, "we will ask God to protect your Papa."

"You believe in God?" I asked, a little surprised.

"I believe in many Gods," he said, "I am Hindu."

"Is there a God for when you want someone to live?" I said.

"Vishnu," he said, "he is the Preserver of Life."

"What do I say to him?"

Taj thought for a moment before closing his eyes and reciting a Hindi prayer. "Shall I teach you?" he asked when he had finished. I nodded. "Close your eyes..."

I bow to the Lord who resides in the hearts of everyone.

I bow before the Almighty God.

We chanted over and over, our voices echoing. With my eyes closed, I imagined our voices rippling in the water.

We were startled by my mother and Dr. Varma who joined us on the terrace.

"Do not hesitate to telephone if anything changes, Mrs. Jones," Dr. Varma reassured my mother.

She nodded and whispered, "Thank you, doctor."

We watched Dr. Varma leave. My mother turned, stared at us momentarily and returned inside. I broke from the others to follow her.

The conservatory was bathed in golden light. It overlooked a vast, green lawn with a shimmering stream, and the plantation far in the distance. My father was reclining in an easy chair, breathing painfully, clutching his handkerchief close to his chest. Without realizing my presence, my mother approached him, my father reaching up to brush the length of my mother's side to her hip, letting his hand rest as he gazed up at her.

"What shall we tell her?" my father said, pulling my mother toward him.

"What we've always told her," My mother replied, "the truth."

"Huh," my father said, a little bitterly, "I didn't think I was afraid of anything. Until this…" his voice broke a little as it flooded with emotion.

"Oh, Evan…" my mother sympathised; she swiped my father's eyes with her thumb and gently caressed his cheek, "Come on, now. We must be brave. For Mags." Her voice cracked as my father leaned in to rest his head on her shoulder.

"Mummy…?" I whispered intently, "Daddy, what's wrong?" I demanded softly.

My father looked at me. He cleared his throat, preparing to speak but broke into a brief spasm. My mother put her hand on my father's shoulder and squeezed encouragingly. He reached an arm out and beckoned to me.

"My darling…" he murmured, both hands covering one of mine, "I'm - I'm going to tell you something, and I want you to be extremely brave. Can you do that for me?"

My eyes grew wide with dread, but I nodded. "Yes. I think so."

"Maggie, I'm afraid, I-I am very sick. And I'm not going to get better."

I frowned. "But… you had an operation."

"It's - it's come back," he explained, flashing a reassuring smile, but I could see his broken heart behind it, and suddenly he sounded ernest, "Maggie… the cancer is - it's in my blood."

"Oh…" I said, giddy with the shock of what I was

hearing.

"Dr. Varma suggested that you are... *too young* to know, but he doesn't know how brave you are. That's why I'm telling you."

My father smiled sympathetically. "But you mustn't worry," he said, "I will be here for as long as I can. I promise."

Without warning, tears filled my eyes, and streamed down my flushed cheeks. I felt the full force of the shock as I collapsed in my father's arms.

My father's bottom lip trembled as he pulled me into his arms, pressing me close against his warm chest. I felt the beat of his heart thumping quickly and rhythmically in his chest like a military tattoo. He fell to his knees with me in his arms, and we stayed there, sobbing as if our hearts were breaking. Then my mother's arms embraced us; her tears flowing now too.

Briefly, I lifted my face to look at him. His skin was pale but flushed, his eyes searching mine as he swept the mess of hair from my tear-stained face.

"I'm sorry," I wailed, "I'm sorry."

My father hushed me soothingly, as he whispered in my ear. I couldn't make sense of his words, but the gentleness of his tone was enough to calm me and my breaking heart, allowing me to catch my breath.

CHAPTER 29

Later that day, I crept into Uncle Singh's library in search of answers to the questions that weighed on me. Deep down, I knew I was probably too young to find them but thought it was worth the risk. In my heart, I already knew my father would not recover this time.

The library was small, but the ceiling was high, darkened by timber walls. I switched on the light, and the room filled with bright yellow gold, showing off huge bookcases, stacked with hundreds of books. I crept through the aisles, tenderly touching the spines of each book on the shelf I could reach.

The books were dusty and well-used. I came across the *Ramayana* and stopped to consider it, but was too focused on searching for useful information to get caught up in the religious text.

Most homes I knew had at least one medical dictionary tucked away somewhere. It was just a matter of finding it. Then at last, I stumbled upon a section that looked promising – rows of volumes heavy with the weight of medical information.

Running my finger along the spines, I quietly recited the

alphabet until – there. C.

I pulled the book free, lowered myself cross-legged onto the floor, and started to read. Page after page blurred, offering nothing I didn't already know. What I wanted and needed was an answer, a cure. But there wasn't one.

Frustration took over me. I slammed the book shut, hugged my knees tight against my chest, and buried my face, sobbing in despair.

That's when I felt it – a strange, cold touch on my shoulder. I gasped at the chill, jerking my head up. Behind me stood a man.

"G-Grandfather?" I stammered.

"Hullo, little Magpie!" my Grandfather cheerfully replied.

"W-what are you doing here?" I exclaimed breathlessly.

"I just wanted to see you, my dear."

"But… you're in *England*."

"I am wherever you are, my love," said Grandfather, "your father will be, too. And I will be waiting for him, don't you worry."

My brows narrowed, and a hot rush of anger surged through me. "You can't take him away. I won't let you."

Then, as if my words had summoned it, a deafening clap of thunder split the air, followed by a blinding flash of lightning that lit my grandfather like a lantern. And yet, despite my outburst, he smiled lovingly.

"You mustn't be afraid," he said, "no one who loves us ever really leaves us."

I stared at him a while, thinking hard. "Is it true that elephants have good memories?" I said.

Grandfather chuckled gaily, "Yes," he said, "I don't know if there's scientific evidence, but I believe it's true."

"Grandfather…?" I said, curiously.

"Yes?"

"When Daddy gets to Heaven, will you remind him to come back as an elephant?" I asked hopefully.

"Of course I will, my love."

He smiled, and suddenly, his ghostly hand sent goose pimples up my arm, and I sneezed. When I opened my eyes, my Grandfather was gone.

"Princess Margaret?"

It was Taj. He had found me. He was standing in the doorway, hands in his pockets, smiling at me. "Are you catching a cold?"

"No, I…"

I looked over my shoulder to see if Grandfather had really gone, and turned to find Taj looking at me with eyebrows raised in concern. "I-I had dust in my nose. That's all."

Taj drew his eyes from me and swept a glance around the room. A fleeting grin lit his face as he plucked the Ramayana from the shelf. "Shall I read to you?"

I nodded, and Taj sat on the floor cross-legged next to me. He smiled and said, "Come! Sit down."

As he read, the hallway paintings stirred to life. Thick streaks of oily paint slid from canvas and frame, pooling on the floor before rising again in shimmering shapes. Rama and Sita embraced and danced with the monkey king Hanuman. Then, before my eyes, Sita's figure dissolved, reshaping into the form of a delicate gazelle.

I woke to find myself in my bed. Taj must have carried me there. Had it all been a dream? Even Grandfather's ghost seemed uncertain now, fading in my memory as my eyelids grew heavy once more. My head sank into the soft pillow, and I slipped into a deep, dreamless sleep.

Morning came with the song of a lone myna bird. I walked to the window and pushed open the shutters. The air was cool and sweet, as if washed clean by a light rain. Below, Mae and Taj tossed a cricked ball back and forth in the courtyard, while Aunty Raksha moved quietly through the garden, picking fresh herbs.

I smiled and leaned on the windowsill. I spotted Taj strolling out into the courtyard munching on a crisp, red apple from the orchard.

"Hello Taj!" I shouted.

Taj halted and looked up to find me. "Ah! Princess! I was just going for a walk. Want to join me?"

I nodded yes, quickly dressed and joined Taj outside. We walked through the plantation, with its tea trees abundant with beautiful green leaves that seemed to light our path like daytime fairy lights. Mae was ahead of us, eager to explore the young trees, their leaves and limbs and everything about them.

"I think we have a budding horticulturist on our hands," Taj grinned.

"Isn't that what you're studying? Horticulture?"

"Yes." He smiled.

"I'm going to be a nature conservationist like Daddy."

"That is quite a mouthful for a little girl," Taj observed, "very impressive."

I beamed at him. The idea of impressing him gave me a thrill of excitement I hadn't felt since I saw the elephant being born back in Africa.

Taj grinned at me and fished in his pocket, taking out another apple.

"Catch!" he said and tossed it. I caught it, a little clumsily at first, but managed to hold on. We both giggled, and I wondered if eight years was enough to make him too old for me; then I wondered… *Is this what it is to have a crush on someone?*

I bit into the apple, its sweet juice filling my mouth as I chewed. Taj still smiled at me, and I smiled back, making the juice run from my mouth. It was a wonderful day.

CHAPTER 30

The memory of my father's diagnosis clung to me for days, its weight pressing into the quiet moments of the house. And yet, life carried on around us.

One bright morning, Mae and I were playing hopscotch along the garden path, the sound of my father's typewriter joining cheerfully with the sparrows, miners and monkeys.

I looked up to watch my father through the window, sitting at his desk in his usual way, with his pencil in his mouth, eyes fixed on the keys, fingers working away like fury.

He stopped; his train of thought stolen by a violent coughing fit. My mother came into view and placed a cup of tea in front of the typewriter.

"Thank you," I heard my father say.

He didn't look at her, he just continued his work as she disappeared out of view. "Mary…?" my father said, less gruffly, still holding a note of frustration.

My mother reappeared at the window, and my father put a hand on her waist, looking up at her apologetically.

"I'm sorry about all of this," he said.

I abandoned the hopscotch and made toward the house. I opened the door quietly and tiptoed up the hall toward my parents' room, pressing my ear against the door.

"You don't need to be sorry, Evan, my love," my mother said, a little surprised by the apology.

I craned my neck so I could just see through a crack in the door. My parents were facing each other, holding one another.

"I suppose it's just, well, things haven't turned out quite as I expected, that's all," my father said.

"I know," My mother whispered.

My father took her hand and kissed it. Then he fumbled in his breast pocket and coughed into his handkerchief. I tiptoed toward them, and my mother pulled me into their embrace. I began to weep at the warmth of the love I felt between the three of us. My parents also began to sob and tremble in sorrow. How long we clung to each other for, I don't know, but it somehow relieved our pain, just for a moment.

CHAPTER 31

Mae and I joined Taj for walks every morning. He thought the routine might lift my spirits and distract my mind from my father's illness, and he seemed to know Mae needed near-constant stimulation. My father said it was a sign of her intelligence, but I wasn't so sure.

One morning, George and Mr. Pang came along. Taj promised us a different view of the plantation, one that, he said, could only be appreciated from higher ground. He led us up a long, winding trail that climbed the mountainside.

The path twisted and coiled like a spiral staircase. Taj strode ahead as our guide, chatting away with George. I couldn't follow their conversation, but it hardly mattered. For me, the climb was a relief and a welcomed distraction from home.

"I suppose you will inherit the plantation, Taj?" George said, a little breathless from the climb.

"Yes," said Taj, flicking George a smile, "but, to tell you the truth, I am not very interested in tea, I am more interested in plants and trees that benefit us."

"What do you mean?"

"Well, of course, many teas have health benefits, but I am more interested in preserving trees for the sake of oxygen."

"Ah…" said George, curiously.

"Just imagine, if there were no trees on earth, all human life would be extinguished. That is what I am learning at college."

"Well…" said George, stopping in his tracks, staring at Taj incredulously, "good for you, old boy."

Taj flicked George a wry smile as they continued walking. A frown creased my brow as a sudden idea struck me. "Taj!" I called, breaking into a run toward him.

"Princess Margaret?" Taj enquired.

"I want you to dig me up a tree!" I said, excitedly, "a young one!"

"Mags?" added George, confused.

"You'll see," I said.

Taj hesitated. "Okay."

He searched our surroundings with his eyes, then fixed on a spot over my shoulder. He approached a young sapling not far from us and dug into the earth around it with his bare hands.

"What's this about, Lady Mags?" asked George.

"It's for Daddy." I said, determined.

We continued up the hill in high spirits. Taj carried my tree over his shoulder, and Mae and I walked hand in hand beside him. He looked like I imagined Rama from Ramayana; we were in awe of him. He was tall and strong with smooth skin over well-built muscle.

"So, tell me, Princess Margaret," said Taj, "what do you intend for me to do with this sapling, eh?"

"Well," I said, "trees give us oxygen, don't they?"

Taj made a face, one that I have heard adults describe as askance, among many other words. "Yes," he said, nodding, "yes, that is correct. Trees do indeed give us oxygen."

"I suppose I-I thought that if Daddy had a young tree growing near the house, he-he might get better." I knew even then that I was naïve to think so. Still, I heard my voice breaking under the weight of my new-found hope.

"Dear Princess Margaret," said Taj, kindly, "you have such a good mind, and a *very big heart*. I'm sure your father will feel better just knowing of your kind gesture."

Behind us, George was chanting an epic-sounding poem. "In Xanadu did Kubla Khan a stately pleasure dome decree… do you know that one, Mags?"

"Which one?" I asked, a little puzzled.

"Kubla Khan, Coleridge!" He replied.

"No. Sorry."

"Oh," he said, and carried on reciting the verse.

I looked up and squinted at the sun; an eagle was circling high above us, hovering in the breeze. The sun's rays making a kind of halo around the bird. It cried out against George's recital of Kubla Khan; soon we all joined in, shouting at the sky with gusto. But oh! *That deep romantic chasm slanted down the green hill, athwart a cedarn cover…*

I smiled and breathed in the fragrant tea leaves. *Is this what Heaven is like?* I thought. I hoped so. With the smell of the tea leaves, surrounded by green and the sound of birds and Kubla Khan… *how could it not be?*

CHAPTER 32

We returned later that day to find a strange visitor at the house. A female elephant stood by the terrace, her trunk outstretched, smelling the air intently.

"Hey!" Taj shouted at the animal, clapping his hands as he approached the elephant. I couldn't tell if he was trying to get her attention or shoo her away, but his voice rang out in sharp, commanding Hindi tones. The elephant stood her ground, turning toward him and letting out a puffing blast from her trunk.

Taj reached up and stroked, speaking more calmly to her now, seeming to ask what the matter was. I walked toward them slowly, my heart pounding.

"She is friendly," Taj smiled, "go on, say hello."

Before I could reach to stroke her, the elephant gave me her trunk and began to explore me, throwing my hair in my face as she breathed. Taj spoke to her, saying something in Hindi that sounded like, "Be gentle."

"She has come to watch over your father, I think," he said.

At dinner time, things were quiet. It was as if a dark cloud hung over the dining room, and no one had anything to say. Occasionally, someone would throw a worried glance in my father's direction, which he quietly disapproved of.

"Would someone kindly explain why you all look so miserable?" My father snapped, "I'm not about to keel at the dinner table."

"We're sorry, old chap," said George, "we're just… concerned."

"Why?" my father said, his voice cracking, "what's the point of being concerned?"

My mother patted his hand. "It doesn't matter, darling," she said calmly, "try not to upset yourself."

My father flashed her a furious glance. Then he rose, forced his chair back with a scrape, like nails on a chalkboard, and retreated up the hall. The bedroom door slammed, and we all jumped.

"Excuse me," my mother whispered as she left the table.

I stood up. "May I be excused as well, please?"

Uncle Singh nodded and signalled for me to leave the table. As I approached my parents' room, I heard the sound of paper tearing.

"Evelyn!" My mother gasped behind the closed door, "for Heaven's sake, what are you *doing*?"

"I'm tearing up the ending," said my father.

"Why?!"

"Why?" said my father, bitterly. "Why? Because we never really know *how* a story will end, do we? It *never* ends the way we want it to; that's for *damn* sure!"

"Evelyn, don't be silly…" my mother pleaded.

"*DON'T tell me what to do!*" my father shouted.

I opened the door, just enough to peep in. My father stood at his desk with his head bowed, leaning on his knuckles on the desk top. My mother stood beside him and the tiny snowflakes of torn-up paper scattered on the floor.

Clearly overwhelmed, my father rubbed his brow heavily, then started to sob into his hands.

"Oh, my love…" My mother said.

My father sank to the bed, weeping bitterly. My mother sat beside him and caressed his arm to comfort him.

"I don't… I don't want to die," my father said through his tears, "I'm not ready…"

My mother sighed sympathetically and held my father close. He collapsed into her shoulder and wept softly. Then, suddenly, he groaned and clutching at his chest.

"Evelyn…?" said my panicked.

My father plucked out his handkerchief, and coughed. He groaned and grunted as he gripped his shirt near his heart and collapsed at the foot of the bed.

"HELP!" My mother shrieked, "Someone HELP!"

I broke and ran. Not for help; others must have heard my mother's cries, because people were already running toward her. Around me, the commotion seemed to fade into silence as I fled the house, desperate to escape.

I tore down the drive, stumbled, and grazed my knee, but barely slowed before picking myself up again. Behind me came the sound of footsteps.

"Maggies!" Mae's voice rang out, but I didn't turn. The river was ahead, and I hurdled myself toward it, driven by something I couldn't name. For a heartbeat, it felt as though I were outside myself, watching the wild figure of a girl facing forward, leaping into the water.

I plunged in, filling my lungs with one last breath. The cold water closed around me, bubbles rising and tickling my face as I exhaled. Then, from the side, came a sudden splash.

I burst through the surface, taking a huge breath. Mae was beside me, stroking through the water, her face tight with exasperation.

"You *crazy*!" she snapped, breathless. "Why you always do crazy things?!"

Her words broke me. My face crumpled, and I sobbed uncontrollably. Mae swam closer, wrapping her arms around me. In that moment I understood, though we were the same age, she carried a wisdom and empathy I had never known. She was the truest friend I'd ever had, and I silently wished she always would be.

CHAPTER 33

The next day, I woke to the sound of quiet voices down the hallway. They were the voices of my mother, George and Dr. Varma. I threw my mother's shawl over my shoulders and made my way into the lounge room where they were all gathered.

"When did it start?" I heard Dr. Varma asking.

"Early this morning," said my mother, flustered, "he was out of breath and then he seemed confused, and he was burning up."

For a moment, no one spoke, then Dr. Varma said, "You may have to prepare yourself, Mrs. Jones."

My mother's lips pursed, as if to stop herself from bursting into tears, and she nodded. I followed her and Dr. Varma toward my parents' room but stopped myself just shy of the doorway, as not to crowd my father. He was lying propped with pillows; his eyes closed, but awake, his body jolting now and then, consumed by a raving fever. Suddenly, my mother swept across the room and shut the door in my face. I stood for a moment, stunned and confusion. I wanted to knock, but somehow thought better of it; I rested my hands and forehead on the door and silently prayed instead.

I could hear the faint sobbing of my mother when I heard my father say, "It's alright, my love... It's alright."

It seemed like hours before the door opened again but when it did, my mother marched out and was met by George and Mr. Pang who hadn't gone far since this morning. She flung her arms around George.

"Oh, George," she said, sobbing on his shoulder, "he's dying..."

Dying. My father was dying. I stood frozen in the hall as my mother managed to gather a little composure; she set her chin and huffed in a very British way. *Keep Calm and Carry On...* I remember seeing the slogan plastered on the walls of the train stations in London when I was younger.

How would we carry on without Daddy? What would be the point of anything without the adventures he took us on? All I wanted to do was hug my mother. So, I did. I marched headlong into her arms and she gathered me close. I expected us both to cry, but we didn't. I felt her heavy breathing and her soft kisses like the pecking of a dove on the top of my head.

We crept into my parents' room where the curtains were now drawn and the room was dark, only lit by the light of my mother's bedside lamp. My father was lying with his eyes closed, his hand resting on his chest near his heart. The room was filled with camphor vapours, billowing from a large incense burner in the corner. My mother held my hand with both of hers as we approached the bed, and I sat beside my father.

He turned to me, at first seeming a little confused. Then he flashed a tired smile. "Ah, Mags…" he breathed, drawing a sharp breath and sighing as if relieved, "good… good to see you, my love."

My mother grasped my father's arm and squeezed lovingly. He covered my mother's hand with his, and they held each other's gaze for a moment.

"Mary… I love you so much," he whispered, with his eyes closed, "you must… You must promise to be happy. We… we've had a good life. Wonderful adventures. I wouldn't have done it without you…" He spoke with short, sharp gasps.

I closed my eyes, feeling robust tears falling from my cheeks and plopping onto my hands. My father drew a hand to my face and caught the tears with the crook of his thumb.

"Be a brave girl," he croaked, swallowing painfully, "be brave for me. Promise me."

I sniffled heavily. "Mm-hmm," I whimpered.

My father smiled. "Good girl."

Then he turned and frowned, looking off into the distance

but at nothing in particular. He grabbed Mummy's hand as if frightened; "it's alright, my love," my mother reassured him, "don't be afraid."

"Ah…" my father breathed, "ah, it's beautiful!"

I remember reading about people's thoughts on what Heaven was like. I wondered if my father was seeing the gates opening, the golden light of Heaven shining through them like light through timber shutters. He made a tiny, gurgling sound in his throat, his body tensed, then he sighed and relaxed.

My mother bit her lip hard, as if she would bite it off, and made a slight mournful sound, so small I barely heard it, but so strong it seemed to pierce the ceiling of tears I must have stored in my soul until they fell silently onto the bed.

My father's hand suddenly became limp in my mother's, and she drew his hand to her lips and kissed it. I was biting my lip now, too, but unlike my mother, I couldn't stop the flow of tears.

The others must have sensed what had happened, for George burst in as my mother stood up. He threw his arms around her, holding her up as her legs went from under her. She clung to him desperately, the quietness of her tears telling of the shock of what had just happened.

I felt as if I had gone blind. All I could see was my mother surrounded by darkness; then I felt two pairs of arms around me, and heard Mr. Pang and Mae talking to me in soft, soothing Malay. I didn't know what they were saying, but felt their deep comfort.

George, Mae and Mr. Pang led me out of the room, but my feet stuck to the floor, and I fought them; I couldn't leave my mother. She had returned to my father's lifeless body; her cries as she touched him reminded me of Elizabeth at Barkings when her mother had lost her baby. My mother's hands swept and patted my father's body as if desperately checking for remaining signs of life.

"Mummy!" I cried softly as George scooped me up and carried me from the room; the last thing I saw was my mother kissing my father's forehead, running her fingers through his hair.

"Goodbye, my love," she whispered audibly, "safe journey…"

George shut the door, and I heard my mother wailing. I gripped George's shirt sleeve hard as silent tears filled my eyes. I made a small sound. I wanted to scream, but I couldn't; I realised my throat hurt. My chest hurt. Everything hurt.

What was Mummy feeling? She had known Daddy a whole year before I had come along. *If I can't even scream, what on earth was Mummy feeling?*

CHAPTER 34

I had never worn black. I did not recognise the little girl in the mirror, in her black dress, hat and coat, and the itchy black stockings. My father's body had been cremated at dawn, according to the Hindu tradition.

My mother was dressed in black too, her skin glowing ivory against the black linen dress and cotton coat. She brushed my hair, but the brush was barely touching me, so distracted was my mother's touch.

Her eyes were downcast, but somehow, I knew she was looking at my hair as she stopped to brush her fingers through it. "You're so like your father…" she whispered, and looked up in the mirror at my reflection and, smiling sadly, she added, "Darling girl."

We gathered at the canal near the plantation to say our final farewell. My mother held my father's urn close to her heart, as I clung to her skirts, hiding my face from the world behind the folds of black linen. My eyes drew upward to my mother's face; she was staring at nothing in particular, her body quivering with grief, which she valiantly fought to control for my sake. She lifted the lid and bent down to me, inside the urn, I could see what looked like fine sand. I swallowed hard, fighting the rising lump in my throat. My father, my best friend who gave me his adventurer's spirit, was gone. Nothing more than fine ashes in a box.

I put my hand in, and a tiny jolt, a shock of surprise ran up my arm and filled my blood as I touched the ashes that had once been the body of the father I loved so deeply. None of it felt real. The only real thing was that my father was gone. The black linen, the ashes, and the presence of the friends around us didn't seem to matter.

I sprinkled a handful of my father's ashes onto the water as the Pandit, the Hindu priest, chanted a prayer that rang through the plantation, awakening the birds and monkeys, like they were joining us in remembering my father.

As the ceremony concluded and guests dispersed, George approached my mother. "I'm so terribly sorry, Mary, my dear."

My mother nodded. "I'm taking Mags back to England." I was shocked by the decisiveness in her voice. How had she made this decision amongst all the grief?

"Understandable," George nodded.

"But I can say goodbye to Mae?" I asked, sudden worry catching me off guard.

"Yes, darling, of course," my mother reassured me.

George put a hand on my mother's shoulder. "He was a fine fellow," he said, "one of the very best."

My mother smiled, the memory of my father almost bringing light back to her face; "Yes, he was," she agreed.

Everyone came with us to the Bombay docks to say goodbye. This was one of the hardest goodbyes I would ever say, I thought. Not only was my father not with us, but I was leaving my best friend, and people I had come to love as family, people who loved my father almost as much as I did.

"Not cry again, Maggies," said Mae, holding me at arm's length before hugging me tightly, "we will see each other again. I know."

"Promise me?" I demanded.

"Of course I promise!" said Mae, surprised at me, "I wouldn't say if I not mean it."

I laughed at her seriousness half-heartedly, but it was good to feel a little happy, and I knew that only Mae could make me feel better.

After our goodbyes, my mother and I boarded the ferry and stood on the deck, waving goodbye as we departed the port. Mae ran down to the pier's edge, waving madly with a smile. I would miss my best friend more than ever.

CHAPTER 35

When we arrived in England, it was raining heavily. Of course it was. We hurried from the taxi up the front steps of our home, and when my mother put the keys in the lock, the door was stiff and swollen. She gave it a good nudge with her shoulder, making it scrape the floor with a strange noise as it opened.

"Alright, my love," she sighed with a sense of achievement, "in you go."

I stepped inside and threw a glance around the house. It was dark and cold, and all the furniture was covered in white sheets. I looked up at my mother, who, just as she was fumbling in her pocket for a handkerchief, broke into violent sneezes, and said, "Welcome back to England, eh? Go and get out of those wet clothes and we'll see what's what, alright?"

I crept up the familiar hall, racing my fingers through the dust on the walls. There were portraits of the three of us, all covered in the same dusty neglect. I smiled at a portrait of my father holding me as a baby. We must have just moved into the house. My mother would have taken the photo; she used to be quite a photography enthusiast.

I heard another sneeze. My mother must have caught a cold on the ferry ride home. I suddenly thought of Florence Nightingale; I had always liked the idea of being a nurse.

"Margaret?" my mother called, "Don't dawdle, please. We don't need both of us down with a cold. Quick sticks!"

I huffed and rolled my eyes. I marched, as ordered, down the hallway to my bedroom. It was dark and covered up, like everything else in the house. I crossed the room and threw open the curtains; the sky was grey, and rain streaked down the dusty window like tears.

No more tears, I sternly told myself as I drew the curtains closed again. I turned and frowned. I turned again, and my father stood in the doorway in his usual jungle uniform, the white-collar shirt with sleeves rolled up and tucked into brown trousers.

He smiled at me. "Hello, my love," he said.

"Daddy?" I gasped.

He raised an eyebrow. "You didn't think I would just leave you in India, did you?"

I shook my head. "Are you in Heaven?" I said, excitedly, "What's it like?"

My father smiled warmly, "*I'm right here* with you. That's Heaven enough for me."

"But…"

"I just wanted to tell you that I'll never be far away," he said, flashing a smile, "if you ever need me, just close your eyes and I'll be there."

I smiled. My father smiled back at me with his broad smile that filled his whole face, then he slowly vanished. He was gone.

"Mags…?" my mother said, suddenly appearing in the hallway. Her voice was thick, heavy with a swollen throat, "Darling, who were you talking…?" I turned to her, and she tilted her head sympathetically as if the look on my face had answered her question.

My bottom lip started to tremble, and my mother scooped me into her arms and held me tight, the force of my mother's embrace opened the wounds of grief inside me, and I burst into tears.

"Come on, now," she whispered, pecking the top of my head with a kiss, "hurry out of those wet things. I'll run you a bath."

The water was hot to the touch and rippled with the light touch of my finger. Steam rose from the depths of the tub, filling my nostrils with the scent of lavender oil; I stepped out of my damp dress and into the water, that wonderful sense of warmth rising from my toes to the top of my head.

A gentle torrent of warm water washed over me from above; I bent my head back, basking in the glorious, refreshing cascade, seeing my mother's face before my eyes closed slowly. With my eyes closed, in the darkness, I heard the call of elephants and monkeys and then, the sound of Mae and me squealing, playing and splashing in the water; I didn't want to open my eyes, and I smiled.

The memory of happiness was strong. We laughed as we worked and played amongst the beautiful song of birds that we had travelled far across the ocean to see.

"Mummy…?" I ventured as my mother rubbed shampoo in my hair.

"Yes, Mags?" My mother said, smiling at me.

"Will we ever go back?" I asked, playing with the sponge in my hands, "To India?"

"Yes, darling…" my mother said after a time, "of course we will."

My nightdress floated down like a great ostrich wing over my head. I yanked it unceremoniously down over my tiny frame, hoping to iron out any creases with the action.

When my mother had gone, I knelt by my bed with my hands in prayer. I chanted the healing incantation that Taj taught us by the river: "And, please God, help us get back to India. Amen."

I stood before the mirror as my mother dragged the comb through my hair, my tangled curls, as usual, causing her all sorts of trouble. I had a habit of fidgeting when my mother brushed my hair; it distracted me from the jagged teeth of the comb on my scalp.

My mother coughed deep in her chest, and I jumped slightly as a memory of my father flashed across my eyes. Then she sneezed painfully, and I made a face as the seed of an idea planted itself in my imagination.

"Mummy…" I ventured, turning to look up at her.

"Yes, Mags?" she said, blinking rapidly, her voice heavy with congestion.

"I think I'd like to be a nurse," I said, my confidence rising and falling simultaneously as I spoke.

My mother must have detected the indecisiveness in my voice.

"Is this because I was silly enough to catch a cold? Hmm?" She said as she looked down at me with a wry but loving smile.

"*No*," I said, "I just think I'd like to learn how to help people."

"Well, I…" said my mother, stopping to clear her throat; "I think that's a wonderful idea, darling. Your father would be very proud of you."

I knew she had doubts, but the little voice I'd heard so much from since the beginning of my adventures with my family whispered that this was the right thing to do. This was my calling.

To prove I meant what I said, I took my mother a cup of tea and some soup, which, as I hadn't yet mastered the art of cooking, was just boiled water and chicken stock. Still, the tea was properly brewed, which I was quite pleased about.

I carried the tray carefully up the stairs, my hands shaking, making the lid on the bone China teapot quiver and the cup and saucer rattle. The soup reminded me of the choppy waves I saw through the portal in our cabin on the ferry, and for a moment, I thought I saw the soup change to the colour of the ocean with swaying white foam.

I set the tray down at my parents' bedroom door and peeped inside. My mother was sitting in bed, and I suddenly saw her image in watercolour paints; she was wearing the summer dressing gown she had taken with her on our trip, with its purple butterflies against the white linen, flitting around orange flowers. Her hair hung over her shoulder in a loose plait.

She was holding a photograph frame with both hands, one clutching a white hanky with laced edges. Her porcelain face was flushed and damp with tears as she drew in a sharp breath, and when she breathed out, she whimpered quietly, mournfully.

"Mummy...?" I said, timidly.

"Oh..." the ghost of a smile lighting my mother's face for a moment, "darling, I'm sorry," she coughed slightly, blew her nose and mopped the tears from her eyes, "I was just looking at this…"

She showed me a picture of her, my father, and a newborn.

"Is that me?" I said, looking from the frame to my mother with a happy twinkle in my eye. "Mm-hm," she said, smiling, "this was taken just after you were born."

My parents were standing outside our house, by the outdoor table and chairs with a beautiful big umbrella shading them. I was in my father's arms; my father was in his RAF uniform, and I was holding his cap in my tiny hand.

"Do you know, you would have been born in India if the war hadn't begun when it did?"

"Really?" I said with a thrill of excitement.

"Yes," said my mother, her eyes raking the sepia photo behind the dusty glass, "Daddy was *just* getting ready to make plans for us to go back, and then…"

"We can go back on my birthday!" I said eagerly, and pointedly added, "That's not very far away."

My mother giggled softly. We would have to wait and see, she told me. But I knew in my heart she needed little persuading. The thought of returning to India stirred something deep inside me. It felt as though being there, walking where he had walked, exploring the places he loved, might bring me closer to my father, to his memory. And perhaps, it might also bring happiness to my mother and draw us closer together, as adventurers in our own right, discovering the world side by side, in his honour.

PART 4

ONE YEAR LATER

CHAPTER 36

The smell of salt, dust, and spice filled my nostrils as we moored in the docks of Bombay. A haze of mist and dust rose from the surrounding shoreline through the beautiful pinky orange sunset.

I stood at the bow, leaning forward with my eyes closed and smiled as I breathed in the atmosphere. I could hear the hum of chatter from the busy people on the pier, workers, passengers and people waiting to embark on their own journey; many of them sounding impatient. India is so full of people that impatience seems a fair attitude to have when all you can see when you are in a long line is the backs of people who won't listen to anything, let alone instructions from more impatient people.

My mother and I hauled our cases as we weaved through thousands of other travellers. I drew a sharp breath to alleviate the stink of body odour occasionally ill-concealed by some essential oil.

Things were not much more peaceful aboard the ship. The deck was crowded from port to starboard, and the noise from the passengers seemed louder than on the pier. My mother and I were pushed aside and shoved forward, and I felt the buckle of a suitcase catch in my hair and pull.

"Ouch!" I snapped, but my cry went unheard above the frantic chatter and shouting, even by my mother.

"Hold my hand tight, Mags, darling," my mother huffed, gripping my hand fervently, her wedding band pressing hard into my flesh, "keep an eye out for George."

My sceptical gaze begged skyward to my mother's face. *Keep an eye out?* I screamed inwardly, and I stood, walking on tiptoe, craning my neck to try and look above the heads all crammed like rows of sardines and crawling slowly forward like a colony of ants.

"Mary!" cried a voice I recognised immediately, "Lady Mags! Over here!"

My mother and I turned to see George shuffling his way to us through the sardined crowd, being most awfully polite about it.

"Oh, George!" my mother gasped with relief and flung her arms around him, kissing his cheek, "it's so good to see you."

"I wasn't expecting you till quarter to!" George beamed happily, "Hello, Lady Mags."

I was in such a mess of emotions when I looked at him; happy to see him, heartbroken at my father's absence, that my lips began to tremble; "Oh…" he said kindly, whisking out a handkerchief, "there now… it's alright," he soothed.

I dabbed my eyes and looked to my mother as she swiped away her tears. She huffed, "Just when I thought the tears had stopped!" flashing George a weak smile.

George smiled back and put a gentle hand on my mother's shoulder. Then he gathered me close and said, trying to help in his upbeat way, "Come on, everyone's waiting for you."

Our arrival at the plantation was cause for a huge ceremony and fuss. When George pulled up the drive, we saw the garden had been decorated to look like Diwali, the festival of lights.

Uncle Singh and Aunty Raksha raced up to our car, throwing confetti of orange blossom and frangipani. "My dears!" exclaimed Uncle Singh, "how wonderful to see you both again!"

Aunty Raksha seized my face gleefully in her hands and showered me with kisses. I felt her tears pooling in my hair; "they are tears of joy and sadness!" she exclaimed in Hindi, which Taj translated for me as Aunty Raksha stroked my face and continued whispering a lament dand kissing me and my mother.

When she had recovered enough, Aunty Raksha said,

"Come, have some tea!"

When we got to the dining room, I was almost bowled over, quite literally, by a flash of colour. It screamed with delight and shouted, "Maggies!" We both hit the floor with a *crack*, which we carelessly ignored, rolling about, screaming and giggling.

I hadn't expected to see my best friend, Mae, but here she was, a year older yet no older at all.

"WHAT ARE YOU DOING HERE!?" I shrieked, and I heard my mother sigh my name playfully.

"My Papa and Tag run plantation now," Mae replied excitedly.

"Taj?" I corrected her, matching her tone.

"Yes, Tags," she said, nodding enthusiastically.

I giggled, rolled my eyes at her, and realised I had never heard her attempt to pronounce Taj's name.

"Princess Margaret!"

I turned and saw Taj marching toward us with open arms. Mae and I charged at him, leaping like a pair of baby baboons. He spun us around, and we swung like a merry-go-round from his neck.

"What a surprise!" Taj said as we leapt from around the great height of his shoulders, "I never thought to see you again, Princess Margaret."

I flung my arms around him and hugged him tight.

The scent of Old Spice clung to his clothes, and he must have had something very British for breakfast; I could smell Worcestershire sauce.

When we had tea, Taj took Mae and me for a walk in the plantation. I was pleased to see that nothing had changed, except the trees had grown and were thriving, and more trees had been planted in the year we had been away; the younger trees were not that much smaller than the ones I had gotten to know, and each of them had their own identity with their own unique markings, neither more beautiful than the other.

"Do you remember when you were here last, Princess Margaret? You asked me to dig up a young tree?" Taj said, looking at me between words to see if I was listening as we ascended a steep hill.

"Yes, I do remember," I said, smiling sadly at the memory of my father.

"Well," said Taj, "I know why you did it, and it was a good thought. I'm sorry it did not help your father, but there is something I would like you to see."

"I thought it would help him breathe…" I said, thinking out loud.

Taj stopped and leaned a moment on the long stick he was using to flatten our path, which was full of weeds and patches of long grass. "Yes…" Turning a sympathetic face to me, he said, "But, he is with God now, and you of all people would know that he would have been most impressed at your knowing about trees and oxygen!" he concluded enthusiastically.

He swiped a silent tear from my cheek, and I felt Mae's arm go around me in close friendship. "Come," Taj exclaimed in a whisper, "Let us go see what I have to show you!"

We trekked a little further up the mountain till we came to a scattering of new trees among older ones, as I had seen when we arrived. Taj beckoned me to him; "see here?" he said, pointing to a young sapling, "that was the spot where I dug up the tree for you."

A new tree sprouted in the spot Taj pointed to with his index finger, quivering with excitement. I gasped and felt a smile creasing my cheeks. It must have been newly planted; its trunk was still no more than a long, thin stem of darkish green with little leaves sprouting from tiny limbs that would soon grow.

"Oh, Taj!" I gasped, "it's so beautiful. Thank you."

Taj touched the top of my head and held it there momentarily as if blessing me; "It is my pleasure, Princess Margaret."

Suddenly, a huge trumpeting sound came, followed by a soft crashing through the plantation. A small herd of elephants was moving slowly toward us.

Taj put an arm out to shield me, gently pushed me behind

him, and grabbed Mae, as she was the most unpredictable of all of us and was likely to run for the hills in terror or run straight toward the elephants to defend us.

Mae grabbed Taj's shirt with both hands, her fingernails almost fraying the linen.

As the beasts approached us, softly swaying as they trudged through the earth, Taj's hand went slowly up and stretched toward the elephants. He spoke urgently but softly in Hindi, soothing the beasts and warning them off.

"Wait, Taj…" I murmured, "look, there's a baby!"

Mae peered out from behind Taj, and I carefully let go of his sleeve as the young elephant calf came tentatively close. It thrust its trunk toward the sky and let out a squeaky trumpet.

We all laughed, careful not to frighten it, and it edged still nearer, smelling the three of us in the air. It had a curious twinkle in its eye, and for a moment, I thought I recognised something.

"Ah!" said Taj excitedly, "it is a little boy!"

I crept closer, holding my hand out for the calf to scent. He drew close enough that his trunk touched my hand ever so lightly. Then he waved his trunk over me, exploring me familiarly.

I squinted at the pupils of his eyes, and I saw my father standing behind me. He was smiling, and the gold of the baby elephant's eye made a kind of halo around him; "Hello," I whispered, touching his little face with both hands, "it's good to see you again."

The calf raised its trunk and trumpeted loudly and happily this time. Then he returned to his exploration of me, and his tiny trunk made kissing sounds on my face and arms; I closed my eyes, and a picture, a memory of my father and me playing on a hill thick with lush, green grass came to my mind. I heard our laughter and felt his kisses covering me from head to toe. *Well*, I thought, *we did say he'd come back as an elephant.*

Then the mother elephant called out to her calf. She was a short distance away, halfway down a hill. I looked up just as she gave another loud trumpet, and her baby broke from me to follow her. My heart gave a tiny heave as I watched the herd disappear down the hill, but I wasn't sad.

"Are you alright, Princess Margaret?" Taj asked kindly.

I looked up at him and smiled. His hands went to my shoulders and squeezed affectionately.

"Yes," I said, when I had decided that I was, "Taj…" I added curiously.

"Yes?"

"I think that elephant calf was my father. Do you think it was?"

Taj offered me a kind, lop-sided smile. "I don't see why not. He seemed to know you well."

"Yes..." I said, looking in the direction of the elephant family, "he did seem to know me well."

As the rain began, we decided to make our way back to the house. I remembered happily that the rain in India wasn't like English rain; it was much more a relief from the heat and humidity than an annoyance.

I closed my eyes, threw my head back, opened my arms, and skipped up the path as the gentle raindrops caressed my face.

"Margaret!" My mother's voice called me in the distance, "Quickly now, or you'll be wet through!"

I burst into ecstatic giggles, broke into a run the rest of the way, and bounded up the homestead steps into my mother's arms; "Oh!" My mother exclaimed, "you look very happy, darling! Tell me, what did I miss?"

"Oh, Mummy, something *magical* happened, I..." but I stopped myself.

"Go on, my love," my mother urged, "you can tell me."

"I saw Daddy!" I blurted out. I desperately wanted my mother to believe me, "There was a baby elephant, and it was him. I know it was because that's what Daddy said. He *promised* he'd come back as an elephant."

My mother pursed her lips to stop the tears from coming, and lovingly swept my cheek. "Darling..." she whispered, "I *believe* you."

She seized my head and held me tight, and as she covered me with her kisses, light as the touch of a newly hatched duckling, I felt tears falling on my head like dew drops from a hibiscus flower. But they weren't tears of sadness. I felt my mother's cheeks pull back in a smile, and she laughed softly.

"Mummy…?" I said, "Do you think I'll know which one he is…? The baby, I mean?"

My mother gazed at me momentarily, then she frowned and lifted my chin to look at her. "Darling… if it's your father, *he'll* know *you*… you won't have to seek him out."

I knew she was right, and her reassurance that my father was with us brought an unexpected calm. It made me realise that in India, among the elephants, my father was with me more than ever.

CHAPTER 37

10 years on and London had become my home again once I decided to study nursing. With a completed degree and a new sense of confidence, I made my way to the London Docks just before my 21st birthday, full of excitement to be returning to India once again. My mother, of course, came to farewell me and was holding on so tight to my arm that I thought it would cut off the circulation. I felt she was hoping it would fall off and remain a keepsake of her only daughter, fearful I would never come back.

"You *do* realise I'll be back before Christmas, Mother?" I said wryly as we turned to each other near the gangplank to say cheerio, "Well before! I don't know what the fuss is about."

"*Promise* me you'll telephone the *moment* you get there," said my mother, with more emphasis and animation than I had ever heard in her voice.

"There won't be a telephone for *miles*," I gasped, "I'll phone you from the plantation."

She threw her arms around me and the force of her

embrace almost pulled me over her shoulder; I had grown nearly as tall as my father, but my mother still stood almost a whole foot shorter.

"I love you, Mags," my mother breathed, "it doesn't matter how far away you go or for how long, it'll always seem like I'll never see you again."

It was the love that shortened the distance of space and time; she didn't use those words exactly, but that was what she meant when she said it.

"I love *you*," I said, flicking a sad smile and trying to stop the tears, "I don't think I need to tell you."

She threw her arms around me anew, "Doesn't mean I don't want to hear it." she whispered in my ear.

Her hand swept my cheek; her skin was older, of course, but still smooth and warm. "Alright," she huffed, sniffing back tears, "go on. Off you go before we both start making a fuss."

I chuckled through my tears, dabbed my eyes and fanned my face, which was flushing rosy with emotion. I still had the handkerchief my mother had made me, and realised I hadn't used it for almost a decade.

"Oh!" I said, closing my eyes as the tears came again.

"Now. Come on," my mother said firmly as she squeezed my arms, encouraging me to get a grip of myself, "you're your father's daughter. An adventurer, remember? You can do *anything.*"

I set my chin, nodded, turned, and climbed onto the ferry for my new adventure.

The cabin was different from the one I had stepped into ten years before, not least because it was a different ferry, but times had changed. The floor was carpeted with a brightly coloured rug, and the walls were covered in artwork and photographs that very much spoke to the bright new decade we had entered.

I dragged my gaze around the room, and jazz music floated toward me from down the corridor. I spread my arms, carelessly letting my suitcase drop to the floor with a thud that broke open the latch, causing my clothes to spill out, and I danced to Mario Lanza.

The ship gave a gentle lurch as it left port, and I staggered, but I didn't care, I continued dancing. Suddenly, I felt someone's hands take mine, taking the lead.

"How good to see you, Princess Margaret," said a deep, rich voice.

At the sound of his voice, I was whisked back to my childhood on the plantation. The years seemed to dissolve, and for a fleeting moment I was once again a child, safe in a world touched by his presence. It was a wave of nostalgia, innocence and loss entwined, reminding me of all that had been and all that was gone. Somehow, the sound of his voice felt like home.

"Taj?" I exclaimed as my eyes broke open, "What on earth are you doing here?"

"I was in London," he said casually, "I was interested in visiting Westminster Cathedral and wanted to see your famous Tower."

"Oh…" Blinking like a stunned rabbit, I said, "Why didn't you tell me?"

"I didn't know how to find you." He shrugged.

Even with my father's love of travel and new adventures, I had never thought about whether or not I believed in fate; I never really understood what it was. But something about Taj's presence in that moment, suddenly made sense to me now.

"You have grown very beautiful, Margaret," said Taj softly, "I hope it is not too forward of me to say so."

"No," I said, slightly breathless as my face creased into a wide smile, "you can be as forward as you like."

Taj chuckled softly, and I blushed bright red. I giggled as the sudden feeling of weightless giddiness made me sway in Taj's arms. He pulled me into his embrace and swept me across the floor once again, to the rhythm of the music.

"I fancied you, you know?" I said, my blurred vision clearing as I got used to the slow waltz Taj had eased me into.

"Is that so?" said Taj, flirting back.

"*Mm*," was all I could manage, "did you ever see yourself when you were 18?"

He chuckled heartily. "I am surprised you knew what it was to desire someone at ten, Princess Margaret!"

"*Hmm*," I chuckled in agreement, "well, I did. I suppose that's the advantage of having parents, isn't it?"

Taj gave a scandalous, playful gasp. "You know, in India, many marriages are arranged? It doesn't matter if you fancy each other or not."

"Who said anything about marriage?" I teased.

Taj slowed down until the music stopped, and I almost lost my balance as we stood there, holding each other's hands.

"I fancied you, too," he admitted, as if I was still ten years old and he was ashamed of it.

My eyes fluttered closed, and I puckered my lips in invitation. I heard Taj laughing softly as he thumbed my bottom lip. Kiss me... said the little voice of my childhood, and I heard the words rise from my throat.

"I would very much like to kiss you," said Taj tenderly, and I was suddenly unaware that I had spoken.

"What did you say?" I whispered.

"I said, I would very much like to kiss you," Taj replied, "did you not just ask me to kiss you?"

Yes, screamed the voice in my head, in chorus with a thousand others. "Yes," I breathed.

I opened my eyes just as Taj closed his and bent toward me, his lips parting. His hand slid up my cheek and around the back of my head, his fingers combing my hair; my heart started somersaulting inside me as Taj's lips brushed mine with a feather's touch, then our lips locked and we lingered in our intimate connection.

I tasted plain black tea, unsweetened, and then a hint of chocolate; I smiled slightly as I pictured him eating his chocolate bar with his cup of tea.

"Margaret," Taj whispered, "will you return to the plantation with me?"

I looked up and my eyes raked his handsome face, which to my amazement looked no different to when I had first met him, even though a decade had passed; there were smile lines across his face, but that added to the beauty of him more than it had aged him, I thought.

I traced the lines on his forehead and swept my hand down to his mouth; they were not unlike a map, each tiny line leading to the plump lips, the colour of a ripe peach.

I nodded; "Yes," I murmured, "of course."

"Maggies?" exclaimed a voice behind us.

Taj and I whirled around, and there, Mae Wen Pang was standing in the doorway, mouth working like an astonished carp. "Ah…" she said saucily, "I am interrupt something, eh?"

"Mae!" both Taj and I shouted at once.

I ran toward her and almost bowled her into the corridor. "What are *you doing here*?" I shrieked, practically excited to tears.

"I could ask you same thing!" she said, pinching my cheeks hard enough that her fingers imprinted red on my English complexion.

Mae explained that she was returning to India to see her father. Mr. Pang had taken charge of a hotel there, and Mae was returning from university, where she was studying zoology.

"*You're* studying *zoology*?" I said, blinking in disbelief.

"Yes," Mae shrugged, "I decide I want to be like Uncle Jones."

She must have seen the shimmer of tears in my eyes, for she swiped them, although a little violently. "Please not crying, Maggies," she said, flashing a kind smile, "Uncle Jones will be happy, and that always make you happy!"

"Yes..." I said, mopping my eyes. I still had the handkerchief my mother had made for me. I took Mae's hands and squeezed affectionately; "thank you, Mae," I whispered, "you're *such* a good friend."

"I know," said Mae, carelessly cheerful.

The bustle of the ship soon pulled us back to the present, and before long we were shown to our cabins. We agreed to meet again after supper, eager to steal every moment we could together.

I lifted my suitcase onto the narrow bed and unpacked, folding clothes neatly into the drawer. I caught myself smiling at nothing at all. The thrill of the reunion with my two dearest friends warmed my chest, and the thought of their return to India together stirred a flutter of excitement within me. For the first time in a long while, the future felt wide open, like a story waiting to be written.

Once relaxed and the movement of the ship settled past the waves to a gentle humming of propellers underwater, I set to work at my father's typewriter, which I had brought with me; I had, of course, inherited it from him, after so many years of begging to use it when I was a child.

It was the most beautiful machine I had ever set my eyes on, and I knew it so well that I didn't need to see it to be able to describe it. It had been made sometime in the late 1940s, not long after the war's end; it was a birthday present from my mother, and many of the letters on the giant metal keys faded with passion.

The ribbon on which the letters were placed before printing onto the page was slightly frayed, and I smiled as I imagined my father becoming frustrated with himself at the tiniest mistake. Never an angry man, he only ever became annoyed when anything to do with his writing was less than perfect.

There was still a sheet of paper rolled into the cylinder, with a page half full of small black letters, each forming words that conveyed my father's innermost thoughts, feelings, and desires for the future, perhaps.

I plucked the grainy sheet from the safety of its coil, and my eyes skimmed carefully downward as I began to read the words. The date at the top left-hand corner sent a shock of recollection to my heart. *October 5th, 1950*. The day of the cricket game. Waves of voices and laughter flooded my ears and filled my mind in flashes of colour to form a perfect memory; the sun shining on the green, making the lawn sparkle. We cheered each time someone had a home run, and George's enthusiastic cry of *Oh, shot* and *howzat*! The words beneath the date at the top of the page read;

Dear darling Mags,

I am writing because I have to tell you something, and I know myself, and you, too well to know that I will have told you by the time you find this letter…

He was right. It was a letter to tell me that he was dying. I could see the letters were smudged in places, and I knew he must have been crying when he read it back to himself. I inhaled sharply, lips quivering, as anyone's do when they're about to cry, but don't want to, and I read on;

I've had some time to think, Mags. I don't want you or your mother to be sad, but I know it's not for me to tell you how to feel; that shows what the three of us have been to each other, doesn't it?

Your mother has been the great love of my life, and you have been everything to me. How I will ever have enough paper or ink to describe the feeling you gave me from the moment I met you, I don't know.

I promise you, my love, all the feelings mothers experience when they meet their newborn baby, fathers feel them, too. So, darling, this isn't a letter to make you sad. This is a letter to say that my love for you and your mother will not die with me, and I hope that fills your heart with as much joy as I have had belonging to you and your mother.

I'll leave it at that, my love.

Be brave. Never forget that I love you.

I heaved a heavy, weeping sigh and swiped at my eyes, which were teeming with warm, salty tears. I looked around, expecting to see his shadow, as I so frequently did after he died, but I couldn't see anything.

I folded the letter neatly and placed it in a pocket of my suitcase. A cool breeze rode through the open portal, and I stepped out onto the deck, stretching widely. Then I turned to my little makeshift desk… *Do you think I could be a writer?* I heard my ten-year-old self say; *You can be anything you want to be, my love.* My father had said, and the words rippled in the air like an Indian heatwave.

I returned and sat at the desk. I wanted to be a nurse, but as I grew older, I found that my fingers ached to be used differently, to be a writer, as my father said I could be, if I wanted to.

How did one begin to be a writer? Did I want to write fairytales or the truth? I put my fingers to the keys and sat frozen for a moment. I fed a sheet of paper into the cylinder. My fingers began working of their own accord, but with enough control that the words made sense as they poured from my imagination like water from a deep, glass pitcher.

I heard footsteps approaching from behind me, but I was so busy that I ignored them. Taj spoke first, his voice far enough away that he could have been in another room; then it was Mae's turn to speak, and my brain made sense of my name, and still I ignored them. This was too important. These were the words I had been holding inside me for a decade, and they held so much weight that I could no longer contain them, and I hadn't realised. My fingers became angry at the realisation. I typed with increasing fury, waking myself from my trance now and then with the jaunty ping of the carriage return.

My heart beat faster, and my breathing became quick and almost rasping. I felt elated. As I wrote, it seemed as if my whole life was flashing before my eyes, the memories becoming words of bold, black typeset, some smudging at the speed at which I typed them.

"Maggies?" said Mae, "Are you alright?"

"Not now, Mae," I said, not even looking at her, so focused on my fingers tickling the keys.

"We should call a doctor," Mae exclaimed over dramatically.

"No," said Taj kindly, chuckling softly, "it is all right. Let her work."

I must have worked a long while. Soon, late afternoon shadows began to creep across the polished wood floorboards and up the cabin walls; the birds that came out at dusk were singing on the shore.

I stopped at last to stretch and rest my eyes. I blinked in the dark, and the glowing shadow of a lantern light crept up behind me, like the earlier shadows that told me it was time to rest.

"It is almost supper time, Princess Margaret," Taj whispered, lightly touching my right shoulder.

"*Mm,*" I said, smiling, drunk from the decline that follows a rush of adrenaline, "I'll take a plate in here if you'll fetch it for me."

Taj laughed softly. "As you wish, Missy Sahib," he said, which made me cock my ear toward him. I had been so used to him calling me Princess Margaret.

"Taj...?" I said to his back.

"Yes, my dear?" he said, turning toward me.

"When you look at me, do you see a writer, or a nurse?" I said.

Taj's eyebrows went begging skyward, and his mouth opened slightly. "What do you want me to see?" he said, confused.

I shook my head, "Just tell me. And be honest," I said, my patience thinning slightly.

Taj huffed and smiled warmly at me; "You can be whatever you want to be, Margaret," he said, "as long as you are happy."

His words sent a shiver through me that pooled in my heart and then spread to my entire body, warming me from the tips of my toes to the top of my head.

"My father said that to me once," I said, smiling, "a long time ago."

"There you are, then," said Taj, flashing a secret grin that felt like it was just for me.

He pecked a kiss on the top of my head, and I listened to his receding footsteps as he left the room; he shut the door, leaving it on the latch, making a peaceful click as it connected to the frame.

Taj had left the lantern beside me, and I turned to stare at its flicker of yellow gold. I tapped the glass. Suddenly, there he was, standing before me, as he usually appeared with his hands in his pockets, his white linen shirt creased from a day's work, and his sleeves rolled to his elbows - my father.

"Daddy…" I breathed in, relieved to see him.

"You found my note, I see," he said as he treaded toward me, his apparition as transparent as glass, but the sound of his footfall so real it was as if he had returned to life.

"Yes," I said, smiling up at him, "thank you. It was a lovely surprise."

"I'm glad," he said with his lop-sided smile, "don't forget to show it to your mother when you get home."

"No. I won't."

"Promise?" he said.

"Promise."

His hand swept from the top of my head down to my cheek, cradling my face, he kissed my forehead.

"Goodbye, my love," he said, sounding strangely final.

"Where are you going?"

Now he was at the window and turned to me; "I'll always be here. If you ever need me, just shout."

"But…"

He disappeared slowly, like mist rising from the ground in the hot sun after heavy rain, and evaporated into thin air.

"Goodbye…" I whispered.

Then I turned. Two tiny white butterflies were hovering inside the cabin where my father had just stood; they were playing, weaving around each other in the air, their wings sometimes touching.

I watched until they found an opening and flew out of it together toward the sky. I smiled. It was just how my father would have wanted to go to Heaven, in the hearts of two butterflies.

For the first time in a long while, I felt a quiet peace settle over me. It seemed all would be well. I had my friends beside me, my mother's love to guide me, India waiting with its wonders, and my father's typewriter, ready for me to write whatever ending I wished for myself.

EPILOGUE

And so, dear reader, we come to the closing chapters of my life. Mine is not a tale of woe, though grief and loss have walked beside me. In truth, the telling of it has been my salvation, a way of holding the very best of it close.

After those precious months at the plantation with Taj & Mae, I found myself in Jaipur, working as a nurse at a local hospital. It was hard work, but it gave me purpose, and in time, it gave me clarity about the life I wished to build. Later, Taj and I married in England before returning together to the plantation, where my mother, now older and in need of more care, joined us beneath its wide, familiar skies.

Yet, life has a way of urging us forward. Once settled, Taj and I dreamed of something new, an adventure of our own deep in the jungle. I longed to write and finish the work I had begun. So, we set off to do just that.

I still smile at the memory of us wrestling with the enormous tent, far too big for two and much too complicated for either of us to master.

"That's the wrong end!" I gasped in exasperation, fumbling with the tent pegs.

"How can there be a wrong end," Taj huffed, his voice rich with mock indignation, "when we do not even know where the bloody door is?!"

"Well, exactly!" I retorted, though I hardly knew what I meant.

"What does that even mean?!" he cried, waving his arms about with a dramatic flourish.

Something about his lovely lilting Indian accent and the way his gestures cut through the heat of the day sent me into a fit of giggles. My laughter soon carried him with me, until we were both doubled over in laughter. And it was in that moment, when the jungle echoed with our joy, that we heard it – a great trumpeting call behind us, powerful and unmistakable.

We turned slowly. There, swaying toward us, swinging his trunk as he went, was a young bull elephant. Taj and I stood stock still and wide-eyed. The elephant did not seem afraid; he came so close that I could almost touch him.

"Hello..." I whispered, arm outstretched, fingers wriggling in gentle encouragement.

The long trunk puckered on my open palm, filling the air with soft suckling sounds as the gentle giant breathed me in. Then, with a sweep that felt both playful and profound, he curled his trunk around my face and into my heart. Hello, he proclaimed, not in words, but in the quiet of his expressive movements.

And in that instant, I felt a gentle breeze stir against my ear, as my father whispered, *Told you I'd never be far away, didn't I?* It was the promise we had made – that we would find each other again as elephants, for elephants always remember their family, always carry the ones they love.

Later, as the fire crackled and shadows danced across the canvas of our tent, Taj tended the flames while I drew my desk and typewriter closer. With the warmth at my back and the jungle alive with memory, I began to write. The words you have just red poured from that moment, and for walking this path with me, dear reader – thank you.

ACKNOWLEDGEMENTS

To my lovely Mum, to whom this book is partly dedicated to, for keeping me in the real world and always guiding me. Thank you for supporting my lifelong ambition. The impact of your love and laughter over my 33 years on earth is hard to put into words.

To Leanne Maslen, my neighbour, friend and fellow creative-writer - thank you for believing in me.

To my surrogate aunty, Helen Cochrane, for her insight into African culture and for always saying it like it is. Your sense of humour and life experience has been a great inspiration.

To my brother, Pat, thank you for being funny, always smiling, and for inspiring some of the characters in this story.

To Jana-Jade Loadsman, for being my advocate and an absolute warrior of an occupational therapist.

And most importantly, to my amazing editor & publisher, Crystal Leonardi. Thank you for loving my little story from its infancy and for your experience, patience, understanding, care, and incredible talent. Without your help, my little book would still be hidden behind the cover of an exercise book!

ABOUT THE AUTHOR

Nadya Radonich was born in Sydney, Australia on November 1st, 1992 to Julie and Grant Radonich. She grew up in the town of Murwillumbah in the Tweed Valley, New South Wales. When she was three, she moved with her parents to Indonesia where her father worked as a Project Manager. She attended preschool there and returned to Australia when she was five years old.

She started writing at a young age, and has a love of animals, a love that was part of the inspiration for *The Elephant Whisperer's Daughter*. She also lived and went to school in Phuket, Thailand for a number of years, and spent a brief period in India, an experience that opened her eyes, and heart, to different cultures.

Today, she lives with her mother, father, brother and three dogs in the village of Nunderi, in the Tweed Valley.

Email: rikkiandmarley@gmail.com

FROM THE PUBLISHER

The Elephant Whisperer's Daughter is a tender, evocative, and spiritually rich story that leaves a lasting impression with the reader. From its opening pages, the story unfolds with a quiet power that is both gentle and impactful.

The narrative voice, told through the eyes of the author as a child, is one of the book's most unique strengths. I love the way Nadya has allowed the perspective to grow with the character, creating a rare sense of intimacy as readers journey through the story. Particularly clever is the decision to begin the narration even before birth - an imaginative touch that sets the tone for the deep emotional undercurrents to come.

The dynamics between mother, daughter, and father are central to the book's emotional resonance. Nadya navigates these relationships with empathy and insight, bringing authenticity to each connection.

The spiritual and cultural elements woven throughout add further depth, anchoring the characters in a vivid sense of time and place and offering the reader a reflective, almost meditative experience.

I thoroughly enjoyed publishing this, your debut novel, Nadya. Congratulations on a beautiful story, rich with warmth and tenderness. I wish you all the best on your new endeavour as a published author.

Crystal Leonardi

Bowerbird Publishing

www.crystalleonardi.com